PLEA BARGAIN

Longarm brought his horses to an abrupt stop. He yanked his rifle out of its saddle scabbard and hit the ground in a running dismount. A bullet whistled past him as he dove for the cover of some nearby rocks. When he lifted his head, another slug sent his Stetson sailing.

"Damn you, Frenchy! I'm taking you back to Denver!"

"Longarm?"

"That's right!"

There was a moment of silence as Frenchy digested this news. "I'm glad that you weren't killed in that courtroom shootout."

"Somehow," Longarm shouted, "I find that damned hard to believe."

"But it's the truth! We're friends! Remember, you owe me your life."

Longarm scowled because it galled him to be in debt to anyone, much less the man that he was sworn to deliver to a hangman's noose.

"Give it up, Frenchy! I know that you're low on water and afoot. You can't win! Surrender and I'll see that no harm comes to you."

"Ha! I'd rather die of a bullet right now than dance at the end of a rope!"

DON'T MISS THESE
ALL-ACTION WESTERN SERIES
FROM THE BERKLEY PUBLISHING GROUP

THE GUNSMITH by J. R. Roberts
Clint Adams was a legend among lawmen, outlaws, and ladies. They called him . . . the Gunsmith.

LONGARM by Tabor Evans
The popular long-running series about U.S. Deputy Marshal Long—his life, his loves, his fight for justice.

LONE STAR by Wesley Ellis
The blazing adventures of Jessica Starbuck and the martial arts master, Ki. Over eight million copies in print.

SLOCUM by Jake Logan
Today's longest-running action western. John Slocum rides a deadly trail of hot blood and cold steel.

→ TABOR EVANS ←

LONGARM

IN THE CROSS FIRE

JOVE BOOKS, NEW YORK

LONGARM IN THE CROSS FIRE

A Jove Book / published by arrangement with
the author

PRINTING HISTORY
Jove edition / September 1993

ISBN: 0-515-11194-5

A JOVE BOOK®
Jove Books are published by The Berkley Publishing Group,
200 Madison Avenue, New York, New York 10016.
JOVE and the "J" design
are trademarks belonging to Jove Publications, Inc.

PRINTED IN THE UNITED STATES OF AMERICA

10 9 8 7 6 5 4 3 2 1

Chapter 1

In the main courtroom of the United States Federal Building, Deputy U.S. Marshal Custis Long shifted uncomfortably against the stiff witness's chair. It was August and inside the huge room, the air was still and stifling. Longarm could feel sweat leaking from both armpits.

"And so, Deputy Long," the defense attorney was saying, "my client and the accused, Mr. Gaston Lemond—known more commonly as 'Frenchy'—actually saved your life last winter up in the Sangre de Cristo Mountains of New Mexico. Is that correct?"

"It is," Longarm agreed.

"And would you relate how Mr. Lemond saved your life?"

"Sure. We were trying to scale a snowy pass to avoid starving to death. I didn't know Frenchy was the very man that I'd been sent to apprehend. He'd given me a hell of a good line and alias. Anyway, we were starving in the Mogollons. We'd already eaten our horses but there was no letup in the blizzard, so we decided we had to try and climb out. I was in the lead."

"But you took turns leading and following."

"Sure. That mountain snow was very wet and deep.

1

Frenchy and I were taking turns breaking trail. We were well over ten thousand feet high with another thousand feet to go."

Longarm's blue-gray eyes tightened at the corners. "I don't know what caused the avalanche to suddenly break loose. I felt the whole mountain shaking. I looked up and all I saw was a wall of white. Next thing I knew I was rolling, and then I lost consciousness. When I woke up, I was buried deep. Funny, but I didn't even feel cold."

"Maybe you were half frozen," the attorney said more to the jury than to Longarm.

"Maybe. I was sure I was going to die. I felt smothered. Like a freight wagon had overturned and was layin' on my chest. I could hardly breath."

"Any idea how long you were buried?"

Longarm shook his head. "At least an hour. I finally blacked out. All I know is that when I opened my eyes, Frenchy was digging me out of from under all that snow. He was shouting and slapping me like I was on fire. Truth is, I was completely numb. I couldn't move. Somehow Frenchy got a fire going. I should have lost my hands and feet from frostbite but Frenchy saved 'em. He was . . ."

Emotion overcame Longarm for a moment. A woman spectator sobbed quietly. Longarm cleared his throat. "Frenchy Lemond not only saved my life, he saved me from being a pathetic figure of manhood unable to take care of himself."

The attorney dabbed at his own eye and when he spoke, his voice was husky with emotion. "Deputy Long, looking at you now in the prime of your life, a big strapping fellow like you are . . . well, it would have been a terrible thing for you to have become physically incapacitated."

"Yeah."

The attorney smiled sympathetically. "Wouldn't you

agree, Deputy Long, that Frenchy Lemond displayed great courage and skill in saving your worthy life?"

Longarm glanced over at Frenchy. "I'd have been a goner if you hadn't found and dug me out from under all that snow, Frenchy. I owe you my life."

"My pleasure," the prisoner said, his waxed mustache twitching with emotion. "I would do it again in a heartbeat, Custis."

"Yeah, I expect you would."

"Marshal Long," the attorney said, competing for the witness's attention.

"Deputy," Longarm corrected. "I'm a deputy. The marshal in this here district is William Vail, that handsome devil sitting out there in the audience."

United States Marshal William Vail, Longarm's boss, squirmed but looked pleased as all eyes in the courtroom turned to regard him.

"Deputy Long," the attorney corrected, waving his hand as if it did not matter. "The point is that Mr. Lemond saved your life knowing your true identity."

"That's right. He saw my badge so he knew who I was and that I was there to arrest and bring him back to Denver for this trial."

"And would you agree that demonstrates that Frenchy has a good heart?"

"Objection, Your Honor!" the prosecuting attorney shouted.

"Objection overruled."

"Deputy, would you answer my question, please? Do you think that Frenchy Lemond has demonstrated, by saving your life, that he has a good heart?"

"Yes," Longarm said. "But that doesn't change the fact that he is . . ."

"The witness is excused. No further questions."

The judge looked to the prosecuting attorney who shook his head. The judge said, "Deputy, you may step down."

Longarm was more than happy to remove himself from the witness stand.

"Your Honor," the defense attorney said, "I'd like to call Mr. Lemond to the stand."

"Proceed."

Longarm watched as Frenchy was led to the witness stand and sworn to uphold the truth, the whole truth and nothing but the truth.

"Mr. Lemond, you heard the deputy say that, in his opinion, you have a 'kind heart.' How does that make you feel?"

Frenchy grinned. "Very good. I try to be kind to people. We're all in this together."

"In your opinion, did you risk your life to help save that of the deputy?"

Frenchy frowned. "What do you mean?"

"I mean, were you in danger of being buried by an avalanche just like the deputy?"

"Why sure!"

"And you knew this at the time?"

"Of course. I was plenty worried about more snow breaking loose and burying me. But I couldn't leave the marshal to die."

"I see." The defense attorney smiled at the judge and then the jury before turning back to Frenchy. "You are a very remarkable and courageous man, Mr. Lemond. No further questions."

The judge turned to the prosecuting attorney and nodded. "Your witness."

The prosecutor was a large, grim-visaged man. He advanced on Frenchy, knitted his brow and said, "Mr. Lemond?"

4

"Yes, sir?"

"How many men have you already killed?"

"Objection!" the defense attorney shouted.

"Sustained."

"All right," the prosecuting attorney said, "let me phrase it differently. Have you ever run afoul of the law before?"

Frenchy looked at the defense attorney who said, "Your Honor, this question is irrelevant and objectionable."

The judge frowned. "Objection sustained."

The prosecuting attorney changed his tack, and in the next quarter hour, Longarm listened as the man cross-examined Frenchy and was able to make the point that Frenchy was a dangerous man.

But the defense attorney did not seem fazed by this as he later began his summation to the jury. "Gentlemen, it is clear that, even though my client was aware that Deputy Long was in those mountains seeking to arrest him, Mr. Lemond saved the very man that would help to put a noose around his neck!"

The attorney let that pronouncement sink in for a moment before he lowered his voice. "Ladies and gentlemen, I ask you, is that the behavior of a cold-blooded murderer? The vicious, demented killer whom the prosecution would have you believe is on trial today?"

No one in the jury said a word.

"So we see that the accused risked his own life to save that of Deputy Long. In view of that, I contend that Mr. Lemond is actually a hero. If not a hero, a man of uncommon courage. He could have left the deputy buried in that terrible avalanche. He could have gone on and no one would have found the deputy's body until late this spring. By then, Frenchy could have vanished and never been brought to this courtroom to be tried for murder."

The defense attorney sighed. "So I ask you to consider

5

this saving of a life when reaching your verdict. Show mercy to my client who has shown mercy for Deputy Long. Know in your heart that a pure killer would never have risked his own life to save that of a deputy sent to bring him to trial."

The attorney pivoted around and favored a pair of buxom young blondes among the spectators who were hanging on his every word. "Gentlemen of the jury, earlier we listened to the tearful pleas of two lovely ladies who have come to testify in Mr. Lemond's behalf. To tell us of his good nature and generosity. These lovely young ladies are praying that you will reach a compassionate verdict and render my client guilty—not of first-degree murder—but of the lesser charge of third-degree murder. This man, Frenchy Lemond, deserves life, if for no other reason than he has spared a life—that of Deputy U.S. Marshal Custis Long."

The defense rested its case. Longarm glanced at Frenchy and then at the two blondes who had come to support the man. They were twin sisters, and if beauty swayed hearts and minds, Frenchy was going to be set free.

But it was now the prosecuting attorney's turn to summarize his case. He came to his feet and glowered at Frenchy's ladies, then turned to the jury. "Members of the jury, it's common knowledge that Mr. Gaston Lemond has shot or knifed three good and upstanding citizens right here in Denver, and all within the last year! And why? Because he has no respect for the sanctity of a Christian marriage. We have seen that Mr. Lemond has the ability to cast a spell over innocent wives."

There was a long, uncomfortable pause. "Simply put, Mr. Lemond is a master of seduction. And when a man's wife is under his evil spell, what can an honorable husband do but to challenge the right to claim what is lawfully his by marriage? And then, Mr. Lemond, being an expert marksman and knife fighter, kills them.

"And so," the prosecutor continued, "while Mr. Lemond is a handsome demon, I trust that you good and sensible members of the jury will not be swayed by his appearance or charm. Mark my words, Frenchy is a monster in disguise! A monster who has killed not once, not twice, but three times! And he will kill again, given the opportunity to seduce *your* wives, *your* sisters, your daughters!"

"Frenchy is doomed," Marshal Vail whispered to Longarm. "Look at the jury now."

Longarm looked and saw what his boss was getting at. The jury, sympathetic only moments before, was suddenly gazing at Gaston Lemond as if he were a two-headed viper.

"Three broken-hearted men assassinated by a professional seductioner and killer," the prosecutor continued, gaining passion and momentum. "Don't let another husband or fiancé lose his life because of that handsome viper. Sentence him to hang!"

The prosecutor was finished. With a sneer at Frenchy, he raised his chin and took his seat. After a long silence, the judge turned his face to the defendant. "Mr. Lemond, you have heard the charges against you. We have heard the defense speak in your behalf. I can't predict the verdict you will soon be receiving, but it is my custom to give the accused one final chance to speak in their own behalf. Would you like to speak briefly in your own behalf?"

"I would, Your Honor," Frenchy said with a formal bow despite the fact that he was shackled and handcuffed. "Thank you for this moment."

Frenchy turned to the two buxom ladies who had testified in his behalf. "My loves, your beauty has sustained

7

me in these dark hours. The mere sight of you is worth life itself."

The ladies almost swooned. Longarm knew them to be the Perry girls, Loretta and Sophie, who worked the cowboy saloons over on Larimer Street. They called Frenchy's name.

"Silence!" Judge Mason commanded, pounding his gavel. "This is not a theatrical company but instead a court of law. Mr. Lemond, address the jury and get to the point! It's hotter than hell in this courtroom and we all want to be elsewhere."

"Of course, Your Honor."

Frenchy raised his chin and forced a brave smile. "Gentlemen of the jury, I apologize for this unpleasant imposition to your lives. As for my own sins, I can only say that no one expects to fall in love. Love comes when least expected and sometimes in a moment of sweet madness. When it strikes, we cannot inquire as to the background of whoever it is whose smile and beauty pierces our hearts. No, of course not! Love sweeps us into clouds of ecstasy and transports us into the realm of angels."

Frenchy breathed deeply, like a man smelling roses. His eyelids fluttered and the Perry girls sobbed afresh. Longarm was both repelled and impressed. Frenchy should have been a Shakespearean actor. He was on stage right now, his performance not for money or applause, but for his life.

"And so, I fell in love with the wrong women. Fell madly in love and my heart was broken three times to learn that they had husbands and lovers. They did not tell me this in advance. Love can be unfair, even cruel, but I blame them not."

"Cruel!" the prosecutor shouted. "You killed all three! What has . . ."

"Silence!" the judge shouted. "Silence or you will be removed from this courtroom by the bailiff!"

Frenchy smiled tolerantly at the attorney determined to put a noose around his neck. "Love *is* cruel," he repeated softly. "I will live every day of whatever time I have left in anguish over the deaths of the men that died at my hand. But I always took their lives in self-defense. So I was deceived by love and then, tragically, forced to defend my life."

He gazed at his female supporters and then his eyes found Longarm in the courtroom. "My friend Custis," he said with a courageous smile, "even if I hang tomorrow, at least I can go to my death knowing that I saved a life instead of being forced only to take the lives of three insanely jealous men."

Turning back to the judge and then the jury, Frenchy said, "I was born with the heart of a fool. I could not help myself for falling in love. Please! Do not still my foolish heart forever."

That was it. The judge excused the jury to its deliberations and called a recess.

"What do you think?" Longarm asked his boss.

Billy Vail was pink-cheeked and balding. He looked like an accountant or bank clerk, but was in fact an excellent lawman who had been promoted into an administrative position that had left him with a paunch. Sometimes he got angry and frustrated with politics and swore he'd take a voluntary demotion and return to the status of a deputy working in the field, but Longarm didn't believe it. Billy Vail was an excellent administrator. Unlike most pencil pushers, Billy understood the difficulties and dangers of his field men because he'd been an outstanding deputy himself for many years.

"Well," Vail said, "I think they'll hang him."

That wasn't what Longarm wanted to hear. "I had hoped that they would show Frenchy mercy, if for no other reason than that he saved my life."

"But took three others."

"In self-defense," Longarm argued.

"Hell," Vail growled, "we all know that Frenchy is an expert marksman and a terror with a bowie knife. So what chance would an ordinary man have against that Frenchman? Especially if he was half crazed by jealousy?"

Longarm had to admit that his boss had a good point. "Well," he said with resignation, "we'll just have to wait and see."

"I expect a quick decision," Vail said. "And a quick death sentence."

Twenty minutes later, the court was back in session and the foreman of the jury stood up to face the judge.

"Gentlemen, have you reached a verdict?"

"We have, Your Honor."

"And that is?"

"Guilty of first-degree murder."

Longarm expelled a deep sigh of regret. Frenchy paled, but then quickly flashed a smile at his women supporters. He would die well, Longarm thought. No sniveling or whining from this man. He would bring down the curtain with flair and élan.

"In that case," the judge intoned, "I sentence Gaston Lemond to be hanged by the neck until dead one week from today at eight o'clock in the morning."

The judge looked into Frenchy's eyes. "And may God have mercy on your murderous soul."

Frenchy dipped his chin in acknowledgment and just as the bailiff was about to take his arm, Loretta Perry and her sister jumped up with sawed-off shotguns they had whipped out from under their dresses.

"Freeze! Everyone freeze!" Loretta shouted.

"What is the meaning of this!" Judge Mason demanded in outrage.

"He's innocent and we're taking him out of here!"

Billy Vail and Longarm went for their guns, but Loretta had anticipated their moves and placed her shotgun to the head of a spectator. "Freeze, or people are going to die!"

Longarm froze and so did Billy.

"Now, shuck those guns," Sophie cried. "Everyone shuck their guns and hit the floor!"

Longarm looked to Frenchy. "Are you going to let them do this?"

"What can I do?" the condemned man said with a fatalistic shrug of his broad shoulders. "Better life than death, eh?"

Longarm couldn't argue the man's point. Like everyone, he tossed aside his six-gun and slid from his chair to the floor, keeping his eyes on the Perry girls as they relieved the bailiff of his keys and unshackled Frenchy's legs and removed his handcuffs.

"Good-bye, Longarm!" Frenchy called, picking up a pistol.

"I'll find you again," Longarm vowed.

"No he won't," Loretta screamed, pointing the shotgun at Longarm and pulling both triggers.

The blast was deafening, and Longarm would have been chopped meat if Frenchy hadn't jumped forward at the last instant and knocked the shotgun upward. Even so, Longarm felt pellets strike his body and saw Billy Vail take even more.

"No!" Frenchy cried, tearing the smoking shotgun from Loretta's hands.

The bailiff, thinking he had an opportunity to be a

11

hero, went for his own gun. Sophie shot him at almost point-blank range. Cursing, Frenchy smashed her across the side of the head and grabbed her shotgun.

"I have one load left," he panted, eyes a little wild. "I want no more blood to be shed but I'm not going to hang for defending myself."

"Give up!" Longarm croaked through a sea of blood.

"I can't, my friend. And don't come after me or . . . the next time I will take your life rather than save it."

Longarm wiped his face of blood as waves of nausea assaulted his senses. Before he blacked out the last thing he saw was Frenchy scoop up Sophie and, with the shotgun still balanced in one hand and the blonde draped over his shoulder, flee the courtroom leaving it in bloody confusion and utter chaos.

Chapter 2

Longarm awoke in Denver's main hospital with a start and a groan. His last memory exploded across his mind and he sat up abruptly.

"Deputy, please!" the young nurse said, rushing to his bedside. "Do lie still and rest. You've been seriously wounded."

The nurse gently forced Longarm to lie back down. His hand came up and he realized that his entire head and half of his face were swathed in bandages. "Am I blind in my left eye?" he asked, trying to keep his voice steady.

"We don't know yet," the nurse replied. "One of the shotgun pellets lodged very near your left eye. The pellets were quite small and our surgeon was able to remove them all, but . . . well, you might have some loss of vision. It's too early to say."

"How soon will I know?" Longarm demanded with exasperation. Then, ashamed, he lowered his voice and gathered his composure. "I'm sorry for raising my voice, Miss . . ."

"Allison. Rebecca Allison." She smiled, a pretty auburn-haired woman in her early twenties with pale blue eyes

13

and a nice set of dimples. She was a little plump, but cuddly-looking, and her smile was warm and reassuring.

"How is Marshal Vail?"

Miss Allison's smile slipped badly. "I'm afraid that Mr. Vail took a few pellets in his neck—thankfully none struck the carotid artery. But one of the pellets did penetrate his lung. For that reason, we have to be very, very careful so that he does not get a lung infection or pneumonia. Right now, his condition is guarded."

"Where is he?"

"In our critical care wing."

"And the bailiff?" Longarm shook his head, remembering. "I saw him fall. He looked . . ."

"He died instantly," Miss Allison said. "There wasn't a thing that could be done. What a tragedy!"

"Yes."

Longarm gritted his teeth, fingered the bandage that protected his injured eye, and tried not to think about the possibility of losing one eye. It would not, of course, mark the end of his world, but it would make it more dangerous tracking down and arresting men when half his field of vision was missing. Much more dangerous.

"Did . . ."

"Did what, Miss Allison?"

"Did those two blonde saloon girls really manage to smuggle a pair of shotguns into the courtroom?"

"I'm afraid so," Longarm said. "As I remember, those women were . . . well endowed. I expect that the bailiff that was assigned to the door had his eyes glued to the wrong end of their anatomies."

Miss Allison blushed and started to leave. Longarm called, "Miss Allison, I *have* to visit Billy Vail. I can't wait."

"He is heavily sedated and in considerable pain. The doctors have strict orders that no one is to visit Mr. Vail until his condition improves."

"Where is that critical care wing?"

"Mr. Long, please!"

"I have to know," Longarm said, his voice taking on an edge. "I've tracked men all over the West, and you can be sure that I'll track down Billy in this hospital. It'd just be easier on everyone if I don't have to go to all that trouble."

"Very well. He is on the next floor up, room number 304."

"Is he conscious?"

"Intermittently."

"Damn!" Longarm whispered. "When would I create the least amount of fuss visiting the marshal?"

"When his doctor okays visitors."

"I can't wait that long!" Longarm's mustache bristled. "Don't oppose me, Miss Allison."

The nurse's eyes locked in a battle of wills with Longarm's icy one-eyed gaze. Finally her shoulders slumped and she said, "Mr. Long, I'll help you visit the marshal's room if you promise to make your visit short and not to raise a fuss."

"How soon?"

"In a few days."

"It has be no later than tonight."

Nurse Allison's hands clenched into small white fists. "Very well, tonight. Late tonight."

"Your word or I'll go sooner."

"My word," she snapped.

"Thanks."

She hurried out of the room. Longarm leaned back on his pillow and fixed his one-eyed gaze on the ceiling.

What a sonofabitch this was! Had Frenchy had any idea that those two blond hookers were planning to stage a courtroom gun battle, killing an innocent bailiff in the process? Longarm doubted it. Still, when push had come to shove, Frenchy had grabbed one of the shotguns and made it clear that he was going to shoot his way out of the courtroom, and if necessary die fighting rather than swing from a federal gallows.

Soon a young doctor came into Longarm's room and said with forced cheerfulness, "How are you feeling?"

"Like dog shit, how are *you* feeling?"

A weak laugh. "Now, Mr. Long, we have to look at the bright side, don't we?"

Longarm turned his head and fixed his one bloodshot eye on the doctor. "There is no 'bright' side to this, Sawbones. And if you don't stop grinning, I'm going to crawl out of this bed and rip your lips off."

The doctor gulped and backed away. "I . . . I guess you really don't feel up to a visit today, huh? Maybe it'd be better if I stopped by tomorrow. Or . . . or better, next week!"

"Suit yourself," Longarm growled as the doctor pivoted and dashed into the hall.

The rest of that day, Longarm fretted and fussed. He could not get comfortable in his bed, and he kept thinking that it was somehow his fault that he had not been able to stop Frenchy and those two women from escaping. On the other hand, he understood that an all-out gun battle in the middle of a crowded courtroom would probably have resulted in many more deaths.

If Billy Vail died, Longarm vowed he would see those damned Perry girls dance on the end of a rope if it was the last thing he ever did—and Frenchy too! He liked Frenchy, but this violent courtroom episode had been the last straw, wiping the ledger clean so that Longarm felt no more sympathy or feelings of debt to the Frenchman.

That evening Nurse Allison brought in a tray of food, but Longarm, despite having had little solid food in the past few days, had no appetite.

"You've got to eat or you'll be so weak you won't even be able to sneak upstairs and visit your friend tonight," she warned.

"All right." Longarm managed a bowl of bean soup and some good bread, and finished it off with apple pie and coffee.

"There," the nurse said when she returned to pick up his tray. "Don't you feel better and stronger now?"

"Yeah, I guess," he told her. "You'll be back later tonight?"

"At midnight."

"Don't you ever go home?"

"I would have if I didn't have to take care of you."

"Oh." Longarm expelled a deep breath. "Yeah, I guess I have been kind of hard-nosed about seeing Billy. But Miss Allison, right this very moment, Frenchy and his girls are putting distance between themselves and Denver. You can bet on it. And I've hunted enough men to know that a fugitive's tracks go cold in a hurry."

"Then why doesn't someone else go after them! Surely there must be plenty of lawmen trying to capture those three."

"Of course. But I *know* Frenchy. He'll find a way to get out of Denver, and I'd bet my badge that he's already on his way out of Colorado."

"Then how can you hope to find him? And especially since you won't be out of this hospital for another two weeks at the minimum?"

"I'll be out long before then," Longarm vowed.

17

"At the risk of losing one eye!"

Longarm didn't like to consider that part of it. He said, "If I'm supposed to lose the eye, then I'll lose it whether I'm here in bed or off chasing Frenchy and those murderin' Perry girls."

"That's not true. Here we can watch over you, keep changing your bandages, and make sure that you have the best chance to keep that left eye. But out on the trail, well, you'd just better ask yourself if two or three weeks is worth half your vision."

Longarm turned his face to the wall. He couldn't imagine being a one-eyed lawman, but neither could he imagine lying around in bed for another few weeks while Frenchy and his girls vanished forever.

True to her word, Nurse Allison appeared at midnight. Longarm was already sitting up in his bed, but still dressed in a pair of damned hospital pajamas. "Where are my clothes!"

"They're in the nurses' supply room."

"Get them."

"Absolutely not!"

Longarm pushed to his feet, the motion making him feel a little giddy. He steadied himself against the bed and started for the door.

"Where are you going!"

"To the nurses' supply room."

"I'll call an orderly!" She grabbed his sleeve. "You promised not to raise a fuss if I took you to see Mr. Vail! You promised you would behave."

It was dim in the room, but there was enough moonlight casting through the window for Longarm to see that the nurse was extremely upset, even to the point of tears. It made him realize that he was badly misbehaving.

"All right. I'll go up in my pajamas and a robe and I'll come back and go to bed."

Her relief was audible. "Thank you."

She found a robe and helped him into it, then slipped her arm around his waist. At six-four he towered over her, but she was strong with the muscular shoulders of a man. It made Longarm realize that the nurse probably had to do a lot of lifting of sick people in her line of work.

"I'm beholden to you for this," he said as they passed out into the dim hallway. "I didn't realize I'd be a little weak-kneed."

"The body, when it isn't used, very rapidly loses its ability to perform. If a man like you, accustomed to physical activity, remains in bed for just a week, he'll lose half of his strength."

"No!"

"Shhh! Yes."

"Well, I'll be!"

"Mr. Long, will you please be quiet! I am not the only hospital person on duty."

"Yes, ma'am," he said as they went up the stairs taking them slowly.

By the time they reached Billy's room, Longarm's head was throbbing and he felt weak and a little sick to his stomach. But he tried not to let on that he was feeling poorly. However, when Nurse Allison pulled a chair up for him, he sat slumped into it before he leaned close to his marshal. "Billy! Wake up!"

Billy Vail's eyes fluttered open. He started badly, and Longarm put his hand on the marshal's shoulder, shocked by how much thinner Vail's face appeared. "Billy, it's Deputy Long. I had to come by and see you. You're going to be fine."

Billy looked up at him. "I know that, dammit! Have they caught those three yet?"

"No. At least, I don't think so. I haven't heard."

"That turban wrapped around your head and half your ugly face makes for an improvement in your looks," Billy growled.

Longarm grinned because, to his way of thinking, if a man could keep his sense of humor, he was going to be all right.

Longarm leaned closer. "The doctors say that you have to stay here for a while so that you don't get pneumonia or something."

"Yeah. I hear the same about you and that left eye."

Longarm waved his hand as if his own injury were nothing. "I'm going to be fine. In fact, I'm leaving this place tomorrow."

"No, you're not!" Nurse Allison protested. "You're going back to bed and remaining there until we know that your eye is going to heal."

"If I've lost it, it's gone and no doctor in the world is going to bring it back," Longarm reasoned.

"Mr. Vail, you're his supervisor! Order him back to bed!"

"Go back to bed," Billy commanded.

"All right," Longarm said, "but if they don't catch Frenchy and his women before long, I'm leaving."

"Any idea where you'd start to looking?"

"A few ideas," Longarm said cryptically.

"Let's hear them."

"Sorry," Longarm said. "They're just hunches and if I told them to you, you'd send another man out to play them. I can't have that, Billy. I've got to go after Frenchy myself. I know how he thinks. I lived with the man in an ice cave for a couple of months. He told me a lot about

20

himself and his past. I'm the only one that would stand a chance of apprehending him and bringing him back to Denver."

"And those two women," Billy said, his voice turning hard. "I want them too! Alive . . . or dead. They killed our bailiff. He was a good man. A family man with two kids."

"I'll get Loretta and Sophie. I swear I will."

Billy Vail nodded. "I wish that I could go with you," he said, his voice thin and wheezy. "But I know that I got a bad lung and I can't."

"I work better alone anyway," Longarm said. "Besides, your ass end fits a desk chair better than a saddle these days."

That brought a smile to the marshal's lips. He gripped Longarm by the shoulder and said, "If those three aren't captured by the end of this week, and if you are up to it, go get them! I'll write you an order for their arrest. There'll be plenty of travel money along with it. However long it takes, however far you have to go—just bring them back."

"Alive or dead?"

"That's right," Billy said, then began to cough so hard that his entire body shook. And when he frantically motioned for a handkerchief, Nurse Allison gave it to him.

"We have to go!" she pleaded to Longarm.

Longarm stood up, seeing the handkerchief darkened with fresh blood. "We're going to leave him like this?"

"It'll pass. Hurry!"

Longarm hoped that Nurse Allison knew what she was talking about. He felt her dragging him toward the door and just before he passed out into the hallway, he said loud enough for Billy to hear, "I'll get them! I promise you, Marshal, I'll bring them back!"

21

Chapter 3

Longarm promised to remain in bed until Friday afternoon, when the head surgeon was to make rounds of all the hospital rooms. After that all bets would be off, he told Nurse Allison.

"The head surgeon's name is Dr. Ronald Payne," she said on Friday morning. "He's brilliant but a little eccentric."

"What is that supposed to mean?"

"He *likes* to operate."

"Not on me, he doesn't!"

"Just be pleasant when he comes around this afternoon. I'm sure that he will remove your bandage and carefully examine the eye."

"He'd better or I'll remove it myself. Rebecca?"

"What?"

"I want to visit Billy again tonight. I need to talk to him about Frenchy Lemond and his women."

"Aw, come on!" the nurse wailed. "I need my sleep!"

"I'll probably be discharged tomorrow and you'll never see me again," Longarm said, taking her hand. "And I think you're going to miss me, despite all the complaints."

Rebecca Allison blushed prettily. "You're a charming man," she admitted. "Rough, but somehow still charming. I . . . I will miss you."

She looked away quickly, then forced a laugh and added, "But then, I miss almost all my patients when they are discharged."

"But me far more than most," he said, playfully pulling her down on the bed beside him.

"Mr. Long!" she said laughing, "If I were found in this compromising position, I could be fired. This goes way beyond professional nursing care."

"I'm sure it does. Would you rather give me a pill or something?"

"No," she said, putting her arms around his neck and kissing his lips passionately, "of course not."

Rebecca's breath quickened as her passions were stirred and when she finally pulled back, she said, "You're a rogue, Marshal Long."

"No!"

"Yes! I find you very exciting, even with half of your handsome face covered with a bandage."

He chuckled. "You might like me better this way. The other half might be a mess."

"I don't think so," she said, her hand running back and forth across his broad chest.

"Will you help me visit Marshal Vail tonight? Otherwise, I'll just have to go up there by myself."

"All right," she sighed. "I'll work the night shift too. I can use the extra money and this hospital can always use the extra help."

"Thanks," Longarm said with a wink.

That afternoon Dr. Payne, with an entourage of younger physicians, came sailing into Longarm's hospital room. Nurse Allison was with them. Dr. Payne was holding forth on the latest theories of infection. He was a smallish, gray man in his fifties, quick and nervous with a high-pitched laugh and the prettiest hands that Longarm had ever seen on a man. Like his protégés, he wore a starched white smock over a white shirt and black tie. His spectacles were round and thick with gold rims. He seemed effeminate, but looked very bright and capable.

"Ah, yes, Mr. Custis Long! How are you today!"

"That's what I'm hoping you'll tell *me*," Longarm said.

"You look good! Color is good." He took Longarm's pulse. "Pulse is slow and strong, that's good."

"What about my left eye?"

"Let's take a look at it!" Dr. Payne turned to posture before his subordinates. "Remove the bandage."

He turned to face Longarm. "Mr. Long?"

"Yes?"

"Close both eyes and do not open them until I tell you."

"Why should I close my right eye? We both know that it works."

"Just do as I say!"

Longarm closed both eyes. He felt them unwrap what seemed like yards of bandaging from his head. At last, when he could feel the bandaging was completely removed, he heard Dr. Payne say, "Doctors, here is where the shot entered. It was a very small and shallow wound and the pellet was easily removed. However, as you can see, it was very near the optical nerve and embedded in this soft tissue at the lateral exterior of the eye socket."

"Can I open my eyes yet?"

"Not yet!" Payne snapped, before continuing on to his staff about how he had performed the delicate operation. He ended by saying, "And so, as you can see, there is no suppuration and it appears the wound is healing cleanly."

There was a long pause and the doctor covered Longarm's undamaged right eye with his hand. "Now," he said, "open your left eye."

Longarm gulped and opened. He saw nothing. Only more darkness. "Aw, Jeezus," he whispered in despair. "It's gone!"

"Not so fast, Deputy. I haven't removed the last bandage yet."

Rage flushed through Longarm. "Then why—"

"There! Open it now."

Longarm opened his left eye and it burned with diffused red light. He blinked and the eye bled tears. He shook his head and watery images sloshed back and forth across his vision.

"Doctor!"

"Tell me exactly what you see."

"Everything is a damned blur!"

"In color? And if so, *what* color!"

"Red. Pink. Orange."

"But mostly red, eh?"

"Yes!" Dry-mouthed, Longarm managed to grate, "Will my vision return?"

"I don't know," Dr. Payne said airily.

Now both of Longarm's eyes were open. He grabbed the surgeon by his white smock and balled it up in his fist. "What the hell is that supposed to mean!"

"Let go of me!"

"Not until you tell me everything you know, dammit!"

Payne tried unsuccessfully to free himself, and that only made Longarm more determined to draw the surgeon closer. "Tell me!"

"Your optical nerve has sustained some damage. There is a . . . a slight malfunction. We don't know what causes such things. I see no inner eye damage itself. No reason why you shouldn't have complete vision. But you must be patient!"

"To hell with patience!" Longarm said, roughly pushing the surgeon away. "I've been patient all week waiting for you to come around and all you can say is that you don't know anything!"

"Give it a day to adjust to the light," Payne urged. "By tomorrow morning, the eye will adjust. I think you may see a great improvement."

Longarm glared at the surgeon and his doctors in red anger. "I'll wait until morning," he said. "But that's it!"

"As you wish! As you wish!" Payne said, retreating rapidly toward the door.

That night, Longarm was still seething and more than a little upset about the fact that the vision in his left eye remained unfocused, although he did think there might have been a slight improvement. Nurse Allison arrived at eleven-thirty, closing the door softly behind her. Longarm greeted her with a scowl that melted into a grin when the nurse unbuttoned her uniform to reveal a pair of lovely breasts that glowed in the moonlight.

"How is the eye?" she whispered.

"I only need one to see when you've grown a pair of tits that big and full," he said.

Rebecca smiled seductively. "Do you think that Mr. Vail can wait a little longer?" she asked, sitting down on the edge of the bed and leaning over Longarm so that her breasts dangled like succulent fruit just inches from his lips.

Longarm's mouth found Nurse Allison's breasts, and his tongue laved each one until the nipples were as hard as dark buttons.

The nurse closed her eyes and moaned softly. She whispered, "I like you even better without the bandages."

"I'd like you even better without clothes."

"That isn't what the doctor ordered," she told him, "but it's what the nurse thinks best."

In a very few moments, Nurse Allison was completely undressed and slipping into Longarm's hospital bed. She was buxom and bouncy and her strong hands massaged new places. He felt her expert touch gently caress his manhood and then his sack, teasing both until they ached and throbbed. His own hands slipped down her smooth skin to find the moist, warm place between her powerful thighs. When he dipped his forefinger into her honey pot she sighed, and then her hips began to move with his finger still inside her.

"Maybe we ought to get real serious about this," he panted, pushing her muscular thighs apart and rolling onto her.

"Yes," she breathed, "get *very* serious, Deputy."

Longarm needed no instructions. His shaft, already throbbing with desire, seemed to have the unerring ability to find Nurse Allison's eager womanhood. He plunged into her like a stallion with a mare, hard, even violent. She wrapped her legs around his waist, shouting vile obscenities in his ear that shocked and at the same time excited him to a frenzy.

"Hard!" she begged. "Harder, you big bastard!"

Longarm gave it to her. His hips slammed back and forth into her until their union made wet, slurpy sounds and Nurse Allison was starting to yell loud enough to be heard all over the hospital.

"They'll think I'm dying and come busting in here for sure," he grunted, covering her mouth with his own as the nurse threw her head back to shriek with ecstasy.

Miss Allison's entire body convulsed. Her legs crushed Longarm's hips and almost snapped his back at the base of his spine. Her fingernails buried themselves in his buttocks and she screamed into his mouth.

Longarm's own torrent of fiery ecstasy flushed reason away as his seed spewed into her body in long, pumping torrents. He had not had a woman in more than two weeks, and he simply could not stop the rush of fluid that emptied his sack.

"Oh, my heavens," Nurse Allison finally wheezed, her legs flopping to the bed and her body going limp. "I can't believe what we just did together!"

"It happens all the time, Rebecca. You just put a healthy and horny man and woman naked in a bed and things like that happen."

"You are an anatomical trophy! If your cock were, say, a fish or a pair of horns, it would be mounted on the wall."

He laughed. "You're crazy as a loon, Rebecca. And I'll bet you say that to all your special patients."

"I don't screw very many, but I saw your cock when you were unconscious and in your pajamas. And I figured it was a prize even limp."

Longarm was glad for the poor light because he thought he might be blushing. Rolling off the nurse, he knelt on the floor, then dragged his clothes, boots, hat, and gun out from under the bed. While Nurse Allison tried to get control of her breathing, he dressed. The last thing that Longarm adjusted was his Ingersoll watch with a gold chain that was also affixed to a solid-brass .44-caliber derringer. He had already checked the loads in his six-gun, which was a double-action Colt .44-.40 that he wore on his left hip, butt forward and ready for a cross-draw which he did as well as anyone in the business.

"Rebecca, I don't need you to show me the way up to

Billy's bed," he told her. "And I guess you can see that I'm leaving tonight. I got my clothes and such earlier this evening."

"You can't do that! Dr. Payne will want to see you in the morning and—"

"I don't think he's got the balls to come back into my room. And as for my eye, well, I heard enough to know that there is nothing more he or any other doctor can do to help. Either my vision comes back after a while, or it doesn't. You're a nurse and you were in the room when Payne removed the bandage and played God. Don't you agree?"

"Yes," she said. "I agree. But I could start working the night shift. Maybe a very good fucking by a very devoted nurse every night would help restore your vision."

Longarm chuckled. "It sure in the hell couldn't hurt, Rebecca. And I'd like nothing better, but I've got to go after Frenchy Lemond and those gals before the trail is stone cold."

"And it isn't already?"

"I don't know," Longarm confessed. "Most likely it is. That's what I'm going to find out when I pay a visit to Billy."

Longarm reached out and laid a hand on the nurse's breast. He took her nipple and rolled it between his thumb and his forefinger.

"Will I ever see you again?" she asked.

"Yeah. I'll be coming around whenever I get a little cough, or a backache or a splinter. I'll check myself into this hospital for a night and ask for my special nurse, Miss Rebecca Allison. I won't let another come close."

"You haven't seen all of the nurses. There are a few that are prettier and slimmer."

"You've spoiled me on lookin' at nurses, Miss Allison. After you, they'll all look flat-chested and under-sexed. You're the only one for me."

She sighed. "Do it to me once more before you go, please!"

He couldn't turn her down. She'd taken care of him for better than a week and given him everything he'd asked for—and more.

"I'm going to go up and talk to Billy first. Then I'll be back down to say good-bye."

"I'll be right here waiting. Please hurry."

"Count on it," he said, feeling his manhood starting to stiffen as he jumped up and headed for the door.

"Billy!"

Billy Vail's eyes snapped open. He stared. "Longarm?"

"Yours truly."

"What the hell you always come in the night for and wake me up? Can't you get up here in the daylight?"

"I'm on a tight schedule, Billy. I'm leaving here tonight." Longarm studied his boss's face. Marshal Vail looked better, but he'd lost a hell of a lot of weight and there were deep lines of suffering etched into his features. "How are you feeling?"

"I'm going to be all right." Billy coughed, but this time there was no fresh blood. "The doctors say that I did catch a touch of pneumonia. I'm going to be in this damned hospital a long time yet."

"I got a nurse friend that I'm going to make sure you get acquainted with. If she likes you, you might never want to be discharged."

"What the hell are you talking about?"

"Never mind. Have you heard anything about Frenchy and his girls?"

Billy scowled. "They just vanished into thin air. I don't think they're in Denver any longer. We've got people watching and listening all over town. Nothing."

"They're long gone, Billy. I doubt they are even in Colorado anymore."

"Then where will you start looking?"

"I'll go down to Larimer Street and talk to everyone I know about the Perry girls. Maybe they had someplace in mind to hide."

"That's already been done," Billy snapped. "First day."

"I'm sure," Longarm said, "but I know a few people down there that owe me a favor or two. I'll press them. Maybe something will turn up."

"And if not?"

"Frenchy has friends too. Someone will have had to help them escape Denver. It's just a matter of asking the right person in the right way."

"Don't beat 'em up . . . unless you have to."

"I never do," Longarm said, feeling slightly injured that Billy felt the need to caution him about such matters. "But I have a way of questioning that is considered second to none."

"Oh, yeah," Billy said sarcastically. "You plain scare the living shit out of anyone that you think has information you need."

"That too," Longarm admitted. "What about the warrants and the traveling money?"

"They're in my office with your file. Ask Henry where to find it."

"Thanks," Longarm said. "How much?"

"Enough to take you anywhere in the goddamn world," Billy Vail said, his voice going suddenly hard with bitterness. "And don't come back without them."

"Dead or alive."

"Dead will earn you a commendation from the Governor of Colorado."

"And alive?"

"The best dinner in town on me *and* the Governor's commendation."

"We'll see," Longarm said, wise enough not to make any promises he might not be able to keep.

"Longarm?"

He stopped by the door and turned. "Yeah?"

"That nurse you mentioned. What's her name?"

Longarm laughed. He plucked a cheroot from his coat pocket, jammed it into his mouth, and headed out the door.

"Hey!" Billy shouted, his voice carrying out into the hallway. "What's her damned name! It gets lonesome up here!"

"I'll talk to her about that," Longarm said to himself as he skipped down the stairs to give Nurse Allison a final, passionate farewell.

Chapter 4

Dawn was breaking over the city by the time that Longarm left his room wearing a black patch over his left eye and a dark stubble of beard. He had caught a few hours of badly needed sleep, but his legs still felt weak in the knees. He guessed that he'd quickly get his strength back on the job.

"Is that you, Custis?" a gossipy neighbor woman named Mrs. Clausen asked, staring at him with disbelief out on the street.

"Yeah, it's me," Longarm replied with a frown.

"Boy, you look awful! You've lost some weight. And what happened to your eye? Did one of them whores shoot it out?"

"No, Mrs. Clausen. I can still see out of it."

"Then why you got it covered up like it was shot out?"

Longarm was in no mood to explain. He flashed the woman the scantiest of smiles, then took off up the street, tugging his flat-crowned Stetson down low over his good eye and hoping to avoid any other annoying encounters with nosy neighbors. It was going to be a warm summer day and Longarm felt a weariness in himself as he trudged down Colfax, past the Mint with its blue-uniformed guards armed with their formidable shotguns. Shotguns not so different from the ones that the Perry sisters had smuggled into the courtroom and used to free Frenchy Lemond.

Arriving at the Federal Building, Longarm mounted the granite steps and passed inside, getting a hard look from one of the guards who did not recognize him with his patch and darkly stubbled face. His steps echoed down the hollow hallways, and he entered the outer office where Billy Vail's clerk sat scribbling notes from a series of wanted posters that he would be distributing to the deputies later that afternoon.

"Good morning," Longarm said to Henry.

"Longarm?"

"That's right," he said, doffing his Stetson and running his fingers through his thick brown hair. "I've come for some travel orders, arrest warrants for Frenchy and the Perry sisters, along with money—the latter being the most important."

"Yes, Mr. Vail told me to have them set aside for you. Hold on a minute and I'll get your folder. It's in the safe because of the travel money."

"Thanks," Longarm said, taking a seat.

"You don't look so good," the clerk said, returning a few minutes later with the file and handing it to Longarm. "Lost a lot of weight. And what's that patch for? Did they have to remove your shot eye?"

"No, goddammit! I still have two eyes, but the patch will keep the eyeball from oozing out and running down my cheek."

"Jeezus!" Henry whispered. "Really?"

"Sure! Why else would I be wearing one?"

"I don't know, but . . ."

34

Longarm wasn't listening. He was counting travel money, and when he finished he smiled broadly for there was an even five hundred dollars. Billy Vail hadn't been exaggerating when he'd promised enough money to chase Frenchy and his girls all the way around the world. The federal warrants were also in good order and they might be extremely useful if Longarm needed the assistance of any local authorities.

"Is there a reward poster out on those three yet?"

"It's in the print shop. The reward is one thousand dollars for Frenchy and five hundred each for Loretta and Sophie."

"It ought to be the other way around," Longarm opined. "Frenchy has killed more people, but always in a fair fight. Those two Perry girls are nothing but busty assassins."

"So I hear."

Henry removed his spectacles. He was a small, pink-cheeked young man who often wore an expression of acute anxiety. Just being around Henry was enough to depress Longarm and make him think that things were even worse than normal.

Longarm folded the money and documents, depositing the former in his front pants pocket and the latter in his back pocket. "Who's been in charge of the Lemond case while the boss and I have been in the hospital?"

"George Dart."

"Aw, Kee-rist! Not King George!"

"He's been working night and day since the breakout."

"But alas, without success," Longarm intoned cryptically.

Henry frowned. "How did you know?"

Longarm couldn't abide George Dart. The man was an officious boor who wrote long and flowery reports and looked every inch a United States deputy marshal. He was tall, handsome, and supposedly related to the English monarchy, and his arrogance was surpassed only by his unfailing incompetence.

To his dubious credit, Dart was a wonderful emissary and Billy Vail sent him to most public relations talks and luncheons. He was a grand speaker, and reflected well on the agency in all things, except his ability to solve criminal cases or apprehend the lawless.

"Has King George announced his daily arrival yet?" Longarm asked with unbridled sarcasm.

"No. But I expect he will be at any time."

"Thanks. Is his desk still in the large office down the hall?"

"That's right. But you know how he dislikes anyone touching any of his papers."

"Yes, I know."

"And he gets livid when you refer to him as King George."

"I know that too," Longarm said as he left, remembering how Dart kept the neatest desk in the Federal Building.

Some people thought neat desks were a sign of an organized mind. Longarm disagreed. To his way of thinking, an organized desk reflected an idle mind, one occupied by nothing of great interest.

Longarm took a seat in Deputy Dart's plush burgundy chair and began to leaf through the neat stacks of notes and papers on the desk. He found a grocery list on top of a list of yesterday's "Important Things To Do." The list, to Longarm's amusement, included such activities as walking the dog, having lunch with Edna, buying the morning paper, and taking advantage of a sale of men's underwear at Henley's Department Store.

Longarm searched the desk in vain for a single reference to Frenchy Lemond or the Perry girls. Nor did he find a name even remotely associated with those three fugitives. There was, however, a scrap of paper with a very amusing and dirty little ditty about a girl from Greece who loved a sailor named Puckett from Nantucket. It brought a chuckle from Longarm, and he was still smiling when King George and several of the other deputies wandered into the office carrying cups of coffee and chatting gaily.

"Well, well!" Dart said, handsome smile evaporating. "Have you found what you were looking for among my papers?"

"No." Longarm did not get up from Dart's special chair. To further irritate the man, he kicked his boots up onto the man's desk and leaned back. "But I did find this amusing little ditty and your 'Important Things To Do' list. Tell me, King George, did your dog get walked and are you wearing a new pair of Henley's underwear?"

George Dart's handsome face colored and the other deputies laughed uproariously.

"Get out of my chair!" Dart ordered.

Longarm pulled a cheroot out of his pocket. He knew that cigar smoke irritated Dart, and that was why he lit the damned thing and exhaled a thick blue cloud of smoke before rising and allowing Dart to take back his desk and chair.

"Have you made *any* progress at all on the case?" Longarm asked.

"Of course I have! My God, did you lose your eye?"

"No, only my patience. What progress have you made, King?"

Deputy Dart ignored him and madly shuffled his papers. He was an extremely handsome man and he must have spent half of his salary on his wardrobe. He looked like a haberdashery window mannequin, and Longarm thought he had just about as much creativity and ability.

"Well," Dart stammered, waving at Longarm's cloud of blue cigar smoke, "I've talked to a few of Frenchy's acquaintances."

"Names. I want their names."

"Now see here!" Dart protested, his voice a blend of shock and anger. "What gives you the imperious right to march out of the hospital into this office and disrupt my desk, then make demands!"

Longarm could have exerted his right by force, but that would have been a serious breach of professional conduct. So instead, he dug his warrants out of his back pocket and waved them in Dart's face. "These have been signed by a judge and they authorize me to take whatever steps I deem necessary to capture Lemond and the Perry girls."

"But this is *my* case!"

"Then close it! Give me the names of the people you've interviewed and then write one of your flowery damned reports and submit it to Billy. By the time he reads it, with any luck at all I'll have taken up Frenchy's trail and be breathing down his neck."

"This is outrageous!"

"This is reality. Give me the names."

"I'm going to lodge an official complaint about this!"

"Fine. Now for the last time, before I pluck your left eye out and insert it under this patch—give me the names!"

Dart's nerve and composure broke. He was not, Longarm knew, all bluff and he would fight if pushed hard enough. In fact, Longarm had once seen him win a splendid fight. Dart had shown he had an exceptional command of the art of fisticuffs and a working knowledge of the Marquis of Queensbury's Rules, which he had supposedly learned at Oxford College.

Dart, muttering, jotted down three names and shoved the list at Longarm, who read them at a glance. "This is it?"

"Frenchy was a loner!"

"Frenchy was one of the most popular men in town! He had friends all over Denver! He was a notorious womanizer!"

"He wasn't so much with the ladies," Dart said with indignation. "And his women were all trashy."

"That may be, but what is your point?" Longarm demanded. "We're trying to find out where he went to hide, not present his lack of credentials to enter the Pearly Gates of Heaven!"

More ribald laughter from the other deputies. King George flushed with anger. "You've had your fun! And while I wouldn't want to fight a one-eyed sick man, I will thrash you soundly if you persist in heckling me!"

Longarm balled a fist and raised it at Dart. "You are the most worthless lawman I've ever seen! Go . . . go walk your dog, you royal moron!"

Storming out of the office, Longarm thundered down the hall and threw a shoulder into Vail's outer office door. It caught Henry eavesdropping and gave him a sharp rap in the ear.

"Ouch!" Henry cried.

"That's what you get when you put your big ear to the door!" Longarm warned. "And when you see Billy next, tell him that I have taken this case over from King George. I've got his three names and I'll be adding to them immediately."

Covering his ear with his hand, Henry grimaced in pain. "Anything else I should tell him?"

Longarm thought a minute, then said, "Tell Mr. Vail that he needs to fire the King before I lose my temper and strangle the pompous fool!"

"I will pass that on, Longarm," Henry said solemnly. "And good luck to you."

"Thanks."

Henry removed his spectacles. "In all the years I've worked for this department, I've never worked for a man that I respected like Mr. Vail. And the idea of some . . . some bloody bitches opening up with shotguns on you and him and that poor bailiff . . ."

Henry's voice was smothered by emotion. Longarm had never seen the normally reserved clerk so upset. Depressed, carpish, and pessimistic, sure. But angry—never.

"We'll get them, Henry. And Mr. Vail is going to be all right."

Henry tried to smile. "And your blind eye?"

Longarm raised his eye patch and winked. "See? I'm only wearing the damned thing because it adds character to my appearance, don't you think?"

"Get to work," Henry said, making a pretense of shuffling papers.

Longarm replaced his eye patch and exited into the hallway. His heels clicked as he strode purposefully down the marble corridor.

In ten minutes, he was on Larimer Street, a collection of saloons, whorehouses, and gambling dens where the cowboys and the wilder hearts gathered for fun and frolic. With his patch and his heavy stubble of beard Longarm would be hard to recognize, and he always made it a practice not to wear his badge except when absolutely required.

The names that King George had given him were of small-time hustlers. Two men and one woman, all petty criminals. Longarm figured that the woman would know

40

nothing because Frenchy would be with the Perry girls and not wish to raise their ire. So that left the two men, Pete Ronker and Charley Sebeck.

"Hey!" he called, motioning over a man selling tin cans full of moonshine whiskey on the corner. "Come here!"

"You want a drink, *you* come over *here*!"

"It's me, Al, Longarm!"

Al shuffled over. He was a bum and a beggar who had lived on Larimer Street for years. As filthy as a street urchin, he looked to be in his sixties, and might have been twenty years younger. "Is that really you, Longarm?"

"Sure," Longarm said, moving upwind of the man.

"What happen to your eye? Some whore poke it out?"

"Sure." Longarm waited until Al finished giggling and then he said, "Al, do you know what happened to Frenchy and those Perry girls?"

"Nope. But I doubt that they're still in town."

"Why?"

"Too many lawmen like you huntin' for 'em."

"Have you seen Pete Ronker or Charley Sebeck around?"

"Charley got drunk and run over by a freight wagon last week." Al made a face as if he'd just stepped in a fresh pile of cow shit. "Poor sonofabitch was sleeping it off right over there in the gutter."

Longarm followed the man's shaking finger and said, "You mean a wagon just ran over him?"

"Naw!" Al shook his head. "You know a horse won't walk over a man. But the driver backed his wagon out of that alley yonder and that's how poor Charley got squashed. Broke his back and he screamed for a couple hours before he passed on. It was a terrible thing, Longarm."

"It sounds like. Don't get drunk and sleep in the gutters anymore, Al."

"Oh, I won't."

"What about Pete Ronker?"

"He's working at the Buffalo Bar. Cagin' drinks and swabbing out spittoons. He's doin' poorly, last I saw him."

"Thanks." Longarm pulled out his wad of travel money and peeled off a dollar. "Take care of yourself, Al."

"Watch out for that roll of money!" the beggar warned. "You may be the law, but if you flash that roll, I'll guarantee you some fool is going to try and kill you for it."

Longarm nodded because Al was right. He needed to keep his money hidden.

Ten minutes later, he strode into the Buffalo Bar and spotted Pete Ronker. The man was easy to pick out of a crowd because he oiled his bald head and then buffed it with a shine rag until it glistened like polished ivory. Pulling his hat down low over his face, Longarm moved through the crowd until he came to Pete.

"Pete, have you seen or heard of Frenchy?"

"Is that you, Longarm?" the man said, wringing his bar rag nervously. "Why you ask?"

"I just thought you might have heard some news."

"I expect he's left Denver with them whores."

"For where?"

"I wouldn't know."

Longarm dragged out his roll. Pete was the kind that wouldn't say anything without a little inducement. "Five dollars, Pete."

"Frenchy was a good friend of mine."

"You'll never see him again."

Pete took the five dollars. "Might be he got on the train and went to Cheyenne."

42

"What would he do up there?"

"Might be he's boarding the Union Pacific and heading west. Going where the deep mines run pure silver and there's big money to be made in stocks."

"The Comstock Lode is about played out. What are you talking about?"

"There's new strikes." Pete Ronker looked down at the big roll in the deputy's fist. Then his eyes lifted to Longarm and he smiled. "Seems to me I heard a name or two. But . . . but I just can't quite remember."

Longarm sighed and peeled off a dollar. Pete's mouth turned down at the corners with disdain and he looked away until the deputy's hand came to rest on his shoulder. Longarm's fingers bit deep into Pete's flesh and the man's eyes bugged with pain.

"To Eureka," Pete said.

"Where is that?"

"Longarm, please!"

Longarm relaxed his grip. "Is it in Nevada?"

"I think so."

"If I find it and he's not there, I'll come back and settle with you, Pete."

"I don't know for sure that's where he went!" Pete wailed. "He just talked about a mining district there. Said it would be a good place for a man to go and disappear. But he talked about France too. So I promise you nothin'!"

"If he went to France, I'll go to France," Longarm declared as he pivoted around and headed for the door.

"You look like shit!" Pete called. "And I'm glad that Loretta shot out your eye! Wish she'd have shot 'em both out, ya big, overgrown bastard!"

Longarm made a dozen more visits that day, some pleasant, some not so pleasant. By sundown he was forty dollars poorer and had not gained a whole lot of information. Still, three other people that he trusted not to deceive him had said that Frenchy and the Perry sisters had taken a train to Cheyenne with the intention of going west. It wasn't much, but it was better than nothing, and the trail was already growing stale.

Longarm bought a ticket on the Denver Pacific Railroad line that ran north 106 miles to connect with the Union Pacific in Cheyenne. The train was leaving the next morning at ten o'clock, and Longarm figured he might as well pay one last visit to Billy Vail and then a much longer one to Nurse Allison before leaving Denver.

Chapter 5

Longarm rode first-class to Cheyenne, up front with the wealthy businessmen, the pretty ladies, and the folks of means. It was an extravagance because it was a short run to Cheyenne, but after his hospitalization, Longarm wanted to rest and regain his strength. The food was superb, the service impeccable, the lounge seats soft and comfortable.

Everything would have been perfect except that, over dinner in the dining car, Longarm was aware that a party of well-dressed people at the next table kept sneaking glances at him as if he were unworthy of their esteemed company. From the conversation that Longarm overheard, it was clear that the two men were bankers and the woman was married to the older of the pair. She seemed the most intrigued by Longarm's rough appearance. Seeking a little devilment, Longarm waited until she was not looking. Then he crushed a grape from his fruit salad plate and slipped it under his eye patch. When the woman next stared at him, Longarm lifted his eye patch and assumed a ghastly, stricken look as the grape slid down his cheek.

The woman's jaw dropped and she stared in horror. She gagged on a mouthful of food and clawed out of her chair to go rushing up the aisle. Her husband, who had been engaged in a lively conversation with his fellow banker, turned and shot Longarm a questioning glance.

He smiled with the innocence of a child. "Good food, huh?" he said, popping the crushed grape into his mouth.

"Very," the banker said stiffly, then leaned out into the aisle to see his wife disappear into the next coach.

Longarm savored his little amusement. He finished his apple pie and smacked his lips, wishing that there was more because he was still a trifle hungry. No matter. A train ride always made him feel like a kid again. He enjoyed train rides immensely, especially on the rare occasions when he rewarded himself with a first-class ticket. He stared out the window at the rolling Colorado countryside and imagined the vast herds of buffalo which had populated this land less than twenty years before. The old-timers who had first come into this country in search of beaver said that the buffalo had been thicker than blowflies on a dead horse. Longarm believed them. He had arrived early enough to see the Northern Plains before the completion of the transcontinental railroad in 1869, and the herds had still numbered in the thousands. Back in those days, the Sioux, Cheyenne, Pawnee, Arapaho, and Ute Indians had hunted at will on these plains, opposed only by themselves and the elements.

That day was gone. The red men were still fighting here and there around the West, but everyone knew that their day had passed. Now, small homesteads were springing up on these Colorado plains like mushrooms. Between Denver and Cheyenne, they dotted the horizon with farm and ranch houses, planted trees and barns, corrals and fenced livestock. It was called progress, and the iron horse had been a large part of bringing it to the American West. Before the railroads, there had only been stagecoaches and wagon trains, and a few hardy hunters and settlers who had moved about as aimless as tumbleweeds running before the wind. Now there was a look and a feel of permanence in Colorado. Good or bad, it could not be denied.

"What do you think about our current national banking scandal?" the banker asked.

Longarm turned away from the window. "What do I think?"

"Sure. You're entitled to your opinion, uneducated though it might be."

Longarm chose to ignore the insult. "Well, sir, I think that the banking scandal is a scandal."

They waited, two wealthy men. "And?" one finally asked.

"A scandal is a scandalous thing," Longarm said, brows knitting in concentration as if he were making some profound statement.

The bankers exchanged glances. The younger one rolled his eyes and turned his head back to the window. The older one, whose wife Longarm had sent fleeing, managed a thin smile. "I agree," he said. "Are you a . . . plainsman?"

"No, I'm a lawman."

"Oh, really?"

"That's what I do best," Longarm said. "Where are you heading?"

"Cheyenne. My partner and I are negotiating to buy another bank."

"How many do you already have?"

"Three. All in Colorado. They're doing very well."

"The only banking men I know are the ones that have made a living robbing them," Longarm said. "Nice to meet someone who actually owns one."

The banker's grin was cool and fleeting. "Excuse me. I had best go check up on my wife. She becomes sick on trains sometimes."

"Sure," Longarm said cheerfully.

He cast a friendly grin at the younger banker, but the man was purposely ignoring him, so Longarm returned his attentions to the passing scenery. He sure liked this northern Colorado grassland. It could be hard on the farmers but it was ideal for cattle.

He let his mind play with the memory of his final night in Denver with Nurse Allison until he begin to feel a cramping in his Levis. Turning his thoughts to Billy Vail, Longarm remembered his instructions to apprehend Frenchy Lemond and his Perry girls no matter how far they had run.

"Be nice to visit France," Longarm said out aloud to himself.

"I beg your pardon?"

Longarm turned to see that the younger banker, a man still in his fifties, was addressing him. "I said that it would be nice to visit France. You ever been there?"

"No, I can't say that I have."

"Me neither." Longarm frowned. "I'd guess they have mostly vineyards. Pretty girls stomping grapes with their bare feet. Things like that."

"Yes," the banker said. "I suppose. Why are you going to Cheyenne and traveling first-class?"

Longarm heard the faintly accusing tone of the man's voice and understood. This rich man was thinking that his tax dollars were paying for Longarm's first-class ticket and that that was a luxury and that men who had eye patches and a three-day growth of beard didn't belong in the nice coaches.

"I'm after killers," Longarm said, deciding to let the

48

insulting question ride. "A man and two women."

The banker's frown disappeared. His eyes widened and he exclaimed, "Mr. Lemond and the Perry girls, I'll bet!"

"How did you guess?"

"The courtroom shootout was front-page news. Let's see." The man frowned. "You must be Deputy Custis Long."

Longarm was impressed. "As a matter of fact I am."

"I can't understand why or how you people could be so blind as to overlook not one, but *two* shotguns those women smuggled into the courtroom."

"Easy enough, considering the size of Loretta and Sophie's tits. Those ladies may have hearts of stone, but they have some of the nicest pairs around."

The banker blushed.

"And as for the first-class ticket, well, I sort of figure I owe it to myself for losing an eye."

"I see." The banker managed a thin smile. "Why don't we forget I began this conversation?"

"No, that's all right. The surgeon replaced the real eye with a glass marble."

"He did?" The banker glanced down at his unfinished dinner. He looked squeamish.

"Sure. Only it rolls around and I can't keep control of the thing. The doctor says that, if I squint, the marble will stay in one place, but instead it just keeps popping out. Wanna see it?"

The man gulped and shook his head furiously.

"Aw, I don't mind!" Longarm said, reaching for the eye patch.

But by then the banker was leaping out of his seat and heading down the aisle.

"Well," Longarm said, reaching for their untouched desserts and smacking his lips with anticipation. "None of them seemed to want to finish their apple pie. Be a terrible sin to let it go to waste."

When the Denver Pacific train pulled into the busy Cheyenne railway station and repair yards, Longarm still had not seen his banker friends again. Apparently, they had decided to stay out of his way. It was late in the evening, and he sought night's lodging at the Grand Station Hotel, one of Cheyenne's best.

"I want a room and a hot bath," he informed the hotel clerk.

The man looked at him skeptically. "It'll cost you a dollar and fifty cents . . . plus a tip."

"Fine," Longarm said.

"In advance."

Longarm knew that the man would never have demanded payment in advance if he had been one of the well-dressed bankers. Irked, he retrieved his badge from his coat pocket, slapped it on the counter, and said, "This is my advance."

The hotel clerk stared at the badge; then his eyes lifted to Longarm's unshaven face. "Yes sir, Deputy Marshal!"

Longarm's room faced the vast Union Pacific train yards and the huge roundhouse where the big locomotives were repaired. Even after dark the train yards were ablaze with kerosene lamps, and Longarm could hear metal being pounded and engines thump-thumping as they were tested and rebuilt. Cheyenne did have its ranching element, but it was first and last a railroad town and the territorial capital of Wyoming, which was even now pressing for statehood. The saloons were always busy in Cheyenne, and Longarm knew that the local sheriff, John Matheson, had his hands full keeping the peace.

That night, Longarm enjoyed his bath and a good night's sleep. In the morning, he had a large breakfast and went to

50

see Matheson in hopes that the lawman had seen or heard of Frenchy Lemond or the Perry girls. John Matheson was in his late thirties, a big, capable man who brooked no nonsense and commanded a good deal of respect among the town's rougher element.

"Hello, John!"

"Longarm?"

"In the flesh."

"What the hell happened to you!"

"I guess you didn't hear about a man named Gaston 'Frenchy' Lemond and his two women accomplices. They pulled shotguns in our courtroom and opened fire."

"No!"

"It's true. Killed a bailiff and wounded Billy Vail pretty badly. He's still in the hospital and on the mend."

"And you lost an eye. What a sonofabitch!"

Longarm shrugged. "The eye isn't lost and I'm hoping to get the vision back, but it's still foggy. If I take off this patch, it clouds my entire vision. It attracts a lot of attention, but I feel better wearing the damned thing."

"Well what about a razor? You feel better wearing a beard?"

"I am on Frenchy's trail. I've already run him down and brought him to trial in Denver once. I guess I'm thinking that I'll have an easier time of it if I look different."

"Well, you sure as hell do." John Matheson dragged a chair over for Longarm. "How can I help you catch this Frenchy fella and his girls?"

Longarm described the trio. He ended up by saying, "I can't even be sure they came to Cheyenne. I'm operating on rumors and hunches. Either way, I need to find out. If Frenchy went south from Denver, I'll be taking the train back down and sniffing out that part of the country."

"According to your description of Loretta and Sophie, anyone would remember seeing them."

"That's right," Longarm said. "And that's all I want right now. Just a sighting and the knowledge that I'm on the right track."

"Where would you like to start?" Matheson asked, picking up his hat.

"At the train depot. I want to know if anyone there remembers them either arriving or departing."

"Let's go," Matheson said, starting for the door.

Longarm was pleased because Sheriff John Matheson didn't have to help him at all. Matheson worked for the county. Longarm was a federal officer. Sometimes locals got real tight-assed about having a federal officer enter their jurisdiction. Not Matheson. The man was a professional without any jealousy. He knew that if he helped the feds, there would come a day when they would repay the favor. It was the kind of thinking that formed a bond between lawmen all over the West.

"So," Matheson said, "tell me a little more about this Frenchy fella."

"Like what?"

"Like what's his edge? I mean, how does this guy get two good-looking women to spring him from a courtroom?"

"He has a way with the ladies. These two are sisters and I guess they just wanted to stay with him."

"A little strange, don't you think? I mean, do they all sleep in the same bed, or what?"

The corners of Longarm's mouth lifted in an amused smile. "Hell, I don't know. If we catch and take them alive, I can ask."

"Do that," Matheson said. "I'd be real curious to know."

"Now *that* is strange."

"We'll keep looking for them here just in case you flush 'em out of some hotel room," Malloy said.

"Thanks!"

Longarm and Sheriff Matheson stood on the train depot platform. Longarm said, "Where do we begin?"

"Well, if I were this Frenchy fella running from the law and hiding in this town, I wouldn't go where you'd expect to find me."

"And that would be?"

"The shanties. The crib rows. Rotgut saloons. Places like that. I'd go to the best hotel in Cheyenne and register under an alias. And I'd eat at the best restaurants."

"With two blond whores?"

"Why not?"

"Fine," Longarm said. "Let's start at the top and work our way down to the bottom."

Sheriff Matheson nodded. "And before we get down very far on the list, I expect you to buy me dinner compliments of the federal government."

"I knew that you had an angle," Longarm said as they started off to canvas the booming railroad town.

Chapter 6

By early afternoon, Longarm and the sheriff had worked their way down through the better restaurants and hotels without anyone saying that they'd seen Frenchy or his girls. Now, as they headed for the rough part of town, Sheriff Matheson's jovial air evaporated and Longarm noted how he kept his right hand near his gun.

When a staggering drunk suddenly lurched out from between a pair of buildings, a panicked Matheson went for his six-gun, Longarm waited a moment for the embarrassed lawman to holster his weapon before asking, "Is there something that you ought to tell me about?"

"Well, I have been having a lot of trouble with a powerful saloon owner named Kevin York. He runs crooked gaming tables and sells bad whiskey. We've had two cowboys die of the rotgut, and hardly a week goes by that someone doesn't turn up dead in an alley."

"Why don't you talk the county into giving you a few more deputies? What have you got now, just one man?"

"He was gunned down last Saturday night," Matheson said. "Someone shot him in the back and pinned a note on his chest that I was next."

"You *do* need help."

"Yeah, but so far no takers. Everyone knows that Kevin York is the one that's behind all this trouble. I hear that he's put a reward on my head."

"What does he own?"

"That saloon just up ahead," Matheson said. "And the one directly across the street from it. A couple of more dangerous watering holes you'll never find."

"Shut them down."

"I'd like to, but York has a lot of pull with the city and county. He makes heavy contributions to re-election campaigns. Gives all the charities a lot of money. He's a real gentleman and slick as shit."

"I've never heard of him."

"He arrived last year with a bankroll as big around as your leg. We have two banks in this town and they were all scrambling to get him as a depositor. The way I hear it, York bought his saloons with nothing but promises. He turned them from losers into big profit makers."

"He must be doing something illegal that you can jail him for."

"I've tried," Matheson said. "Three times. And every time I thought I had a good witness to haul before the judge, the witness either disappeared or was murdered."

"It sounds pretty bad," Longarm said. "I'd like to pay this York fella a little visit. Maybe we could get something federal on him that I can investigate."

"Not likely. York is too clever for that. Most likely, he'll keep piling up big profits until some drunken cowboy or whore pulls a gun and drills a hole in his gizzard. That's what often happens to that kind of fella. They have bodyguards and take all the precautions, but they can never predict when someone completely unexpected will fly into a rage and take their life."

At the entrance to Kevin York's Wild Goose Saloon,

57

Sheriff Matheson took a deep breath and then led the way inside. The place was doing a good business that would probably get even better before the night passed. The bar itself was fancy and polished to a shine. Ornately carved, it stretched forty feet across the south end of the big saloon, and three bartenders were required to handle the seventy or eighty thirsty cowboys, railroad workers, and laborers. In the middle of the saloon were an even dozen gambling tables, four of which were still draped in readiness for the heavier business that would come after dark.

"Pretty nice place for this part of town," Longarm observed.

"You haven't seen the *real* draw yet," Matheson said. He pulled his pocket watch out of his vest, consulted it for a moment, and said, "It's five-forty-six. We'll have a beer and wait."

"For what?"

"You'll see."

Longarm shrugged and followed the sheriff over to the bar. Matheson called, "Two beers. And don't give us any of that watery green piss. I want the real brewery beer."

The bartender, a sweaty young man in a bowler hat, nodded grimly. He brought two mugs of beer, and it was good. Matheson and Longarm turned around, hooked their elbows on the bar, and sipped at the foam.

"How does York do it?" Longarm asked.

"You mean get so many people in here?"

"Yeah."

"You'll see pretty quick."

Longarm did not like guessing games, but Matheson had bought the beer and he'd be happy enough to wait a few more minutes.

"Uh-oh," the sheriff said, stiffening. "Here comes the smooth-talking devil himself. Just stay out of this. In fact, it would be better if York doesn't realize you're a deputy United States Marshal."

"Well I sure as hell ain't ashamed of that," Longarm growled.

Kevin York looked like a younger version of the bankers Longarm had driven out of the railroad dining car. The man was dressed very well but also very conservatively. Slender and graceful, Kevin York was of average height, with a prominent jaw and wearing a diamond stickpin, black suit, and blue tie. He was prosperous and respectable-looking. Longarm noted how the man's eyes constantly moved back and forth surveying his flourishing business. He never looked directly at Sheriff Matheson or in any way acknowledged his presence. Smiling, shaking his customers' hands, with a pat on the back here, a quick joke followed by laughter there, he had the polish of a highly successful politician.

York worked the room for five minutes before he finally reached the bar, and even then he was still smiling. He raised his hand in signal, and a bartender found a very special brand of whiskey under the counter and a special glass of cut crystal was quickly filled.

"Well, well, Sheriff," York said cheerfully. "Have you come to tell me that you are going to mend your ways and cooperate with Cheyenne's next mayor?"

"No, I came to have a beer and to see the show. And maybe to tell you that I have every intention of nailing your hide to the wall one fine day."

York chuckled. "Sheriff, it's a good thing that you are a man without a wife and children. Without a future. You see, I'm afraid that I've heard rumors about your impending demise."

"Is that right?" Matheson said with a hard edge to his voice.

"Oh, yes! It's a pity a man like you won't be reasonable. Won't learn to work with the system instead of fight it. You know, I could use another good man with a gun to protect me from my competitors."

Matheson's eyes flicked to three men in the crowd who were standing motionless and tensed. "You've got enough hired guns already."

"Yes," York said, sipping his whiskey, cold eyes leveled over his glass and twice flicking at Longarm. "And I think it's about time that they earned their wages."

"Anytime they want," Matheson grated, his eyes flinty and unyielding.

The sheriff was about to say something else, but his voice was drowned out by a bugle and a drum roll. Longarm twisted around to see a beautiful and scantily clad woman dash out from behind a curtain with a huge black bear. The lumbering beast looked to be smiling as it was led forward on a brass chain and wearing a sequined collar. The crowd erupted in applause and cheers.

"What in God's name is this?" Longarm muttered.

"*This* is what brings the crowds in," the sheriff replied. "Watch."

Longarm stood dumbfounded as the bugler trotted over to a piano and began to play while the drummer picked up a fiddle and joined him in a duet. Together, they managed to play a waltz while the woman pressed her bosom to the hairy chest of the black bear, took its paws in her hands, and began to dance.

They were good! Longarm's jaw dropped and the crowd cheered as the bear, with its tongue lolling out the side of its mouth and drooling on the woman, danced around and around to the music.

"Well I'll be damned!" Longarm said. "That's something I won't soon forget. Do they do anything else?"

"Yeah," Matheson said, not looking very happy. "But I haven't caught them doing it yet. When I do, I'll put Mr. York here out of business."

"On what charge?" the saloon owner asked.

"I'll think of one. And if I can't, you can bet that I'll make one up."

Even as Longarm stared, he could see that the big black bear was getting a mammoth erection that could not be concealed even by his long black belly hair. The crowd, on seeing this, began to hoot and scream with delight. The bear turned glassy-eyed and started hopping up and down rather than shuffling in a circle. Just when Longarm thought the beast was going to stop dancing and get amorous, the waltz ended.

The crowd cheered uproariously. The woman dragged her bear off the stage and into the wings while everyone laughed and some even threw coins to show their appreciation.

"Well I'll be damned!" Longarm said. "I never saw anything like that."

"Neither has anyone else," Matheson said sourly. "The woman and the bear are on their way to York's other saloon. They dance every half hour, alternating from one side of the street to the other. In about fifteen minutes, this place will empty across the street to order fresh drinks at York's other saloon."

"That's right," York said, looking like a cat who'd swallowed a mouse. "They just go charging back and forth, all night long."

"The act will wear thin," Matheson said. "And when it does, what will you do then?"

"I'll be even wealthier and you'll be dead," York said with a thin smile.

He started to leave, but the sheriff grabbed him by the sleeve. "I could jail you for threatening me!"

"And I'd post bail and you'd look even more the bumbling fool," York said, his smile frozen in place. "Face it, you're on the losing side."

"And you're on the winning side?"

"Hell, yes! Look around! I'm already the wealthiest man in Cheyenne. I'll become mayor and then I'll get you fired, Sheriff."

"We'll see about that," Matheson grated.

He released his grip and turned away to call for a whiskey. Catching the reflection of Matheson's face in the back bar mirror, Longarm could see that his friend looked confused and defeated.

"Leave the bottle," Matheson said. "Mr. Long is paying for it."

Longarm paid. They drank in silence until the dancing girl and the horny black bear returned and began to dance again at seven o'clock, and then the lawmen left in a tense silence.

"You got a problem there," Longarm said.

"I know that."

"York as much as promised he'd have you gunned down. What are you waiting for?"

"You mean, why don't I force a showdown?"

"Yeah. Better on your terms than on a backshooter's."

Matheson stopped in his tracks. "Are you saying I should just go up to the man, force him to draw, and kill him?"

"Something like that." Longarm toed the dirt of the street. "You'll be shot down if you don't do something, John."

"But you saw his hired gunmen."

"Yes, I did. And I say we go back into that saloon and

clean them out right now. Then we shut down the man's saloon."

"On what charges?"

Longarm thought a moment. "Unusual cruelty to an animal."

"That's a charge?"

"Sure! Look at it this way. If you saw a man take a club to a horse and beat it to death, wouldn't you stop and arrest him before he killed the dumb beast?"

"Well, of course, but that bear looks like it *enjoys* dancing with the woman."

"No, no!" Longarm said quickly. "That wasn't a grin on its face."

"It wasn't?

"Of course not!"

"Looked to me like a grin."

"It wasn't," Longarm assured his friend. "That animal wants to screw that woman so damned bad he's in agony. Anyone can see that. Put yourself in the bear's position! And wasn't it drooling all over her?"

"Yeah, but . . ."

"Cruelty to animals is a criminal offense," Longarm said.

"It is?"

"That's right. And since that animal has probably been transported across state lines, it's a federal offense."

Longarm retrieved his badge from his pocket and pinned it on his coat. "Let's go make our arrest."

"I . . . well, I don't know about this," Matheson hedged.

"Better now than later when I'm gone and you're up against them all by yourself."

John Matheson expelled a deep breath. "Yeah," he said. "But you sure don't need to buy into this. The deck is pretty well stacked against us."

Longarm patted his gun and gave his worried friend a reassuring smile. "If bullets start to fly, let's do our best not to kill the bear. Okay?"

"Okay!"

And so they wheeled about and went back into the saloon.

Chapter 7

When Kevin York saw the federal deputy's badge now pinned on Longarm's chest, he realized that there was big trouble heading in his direction. He barked an order to his gunmen and started to reach behind the bar.

"Freeze!" Sheriff Matheson shouted, drawing his sixgun. "York, you're under arrest!" The saloon fell silent, and the woman and bear stopped dancing.

The wealthy saloon owner froze, turned back, and managed a smile. "On what charge?"

Matheson cast a glance at Longarm, who nodded with encouragement. The sheriff cleared his throat and said loud enough for everyone in the Wild Goose to hear, "Cruelty to dumb animals."

"What!"

"The bear, goddammit!"

"What's cruel about him dancing with a pretty woman!" York turned to point at the woman and the bear. "Look at him! That bear is grinning!"

"He's horny! He wants to do more than dance."

"Jeezus!" York exclaimed, throwing his hands skyward with exasperation. "I don't believe my ears. You're going to arrest me because you think the bear is . . . is hot for his dance partner?"

Even Longarm, trying to keep his eyes on York's three gunmen, had to admit the charge sounded laughable. The saloon patrons began to snicker, and this made the sheriff blush deeply, but he was in too far now to do a turnabout so he said, "You're arrested and so is the woman and the bear."

The crowd began to hoot with derision. Longarm could see that Matheson was sweating profusely. He knew that he could no longer remain detached but had to step in and rescue the beleaguered sheriff.

Addressing Kevin York, he said, "My name is Deputy Long. I'm a federal officer and I believe that there is a federal offense being committed here in respect to the bear."

"You are both idiots!" York shouted. "And I'll be damned if I'm going to be arrested on some ridiculous charge of cruelty to that bear. Why, I've never seen a happier bear!"

York turned to his sympathetic patrons. "Does anyone else think that black bear is unhappy? Take a good look at him!"

The crowd left no doubt they thought that the bear was indeed very happy.

Matheson leaned closer to Longarm. "This is getting out of control. I'll get the handcuffs on York. You arrest the girl and the bear."

"Thanks," Longarm said. "But we've got three more pressing problems."

Sheriff Matheson followed Longarm's gaze and understood. York's trio of hired guns had moved apart and were taking advantageous firing positions. The sheriff's eyes returned to Kevin York. "You'd better tell your gunmen

66

to take a walk or a lot of people are going to go down."

"Starting with you, Sheriff."

York raised his hands shoulder high, leaving no doubt that he was out of the fray. "Boys," he said, "you're fired. You don't work for me as of right now. But I still expect you to do what is right and best for your own future."

Longarm understood what was going on. Kevin York had just covered his ass in a court of law. After publicly firing his gunmen, he could no longer be held responsible for what was about to happen. And yet, he'd made it very clear to his three gunmen that their loyalty was expected.

Longarm turned to the three men as the saloon began to empty in a rush for the door. "You boys have just been fired. I expect you'll show good sense and leave with everyone else."

But one of them, a thin, pocked-faced man in his twenties, shook his head. "It ain't right to arrest Mr. York and the bear. The bear is happy. We were all happy until you two interfered."

"Leave now," Longarm said quietly. "It's the last warning you'll get."

But the thin man just smiled. His eyes flicked to the pair of men flanking him, and he looked very confident when he said, "Make your play, or tuck your tail between your legs and crawl outa here fast."

Longarm could see Sheriff Matheson shifting his feet just slightly toward the three and he said, "I'll take the two on the left, you go for the one on the right."

"And Mr. York?"

"Whoever finishes first can put a bullet in him."

York's smile melted. He nervously licked his thin lips. "Maybe we can work this out without bloodshed. Maybe a little money would help us come to a more reasonable accommodation."

"You're under arrest for cruelty to animals. The girl is under arrest and so is your goddamn bear!" Matheson snarled.

York took a deep breath and pressed the small of his back against the bar. And then, almost imperceptibly, he gave a shallow nod of his chin.

Longarm sensed the play and his right hand had only a few inches to travel as it streaked across his belly and found the exposed butt of his gun. His cross-draw was smooth and without any wasted motion. His gun came out and automatically sought the faster of the two men he faced as it bucked in his big fist. His bullet knocked the thin gunfighter over a faro table sending cards and chips flying. His next bullet dutifully took out his second target, a nondescript gunman whose only distinguishing feature was a knife scar that had clipped off most of his right ear. But this man was quick, and even as Longarm's bullet punched him a step backward, the man's gun bucked and a slug ate wood in the bar less than an inch from Longarm.

Sheriff Matheson wasn't a fast gun. His Colt belched fire and smoke against incoming fire and smoke. Shots blended, and Longarm wasn't certain who would fall as he swung his own smoking Colt tracking toward Kevin York. The saloon owner had reacted with lightning speed and yanked a shotgun up from behind the polished bartop.

Longarm felt a river colder than ice shoot through his body. He even froze for an instant remembering the last time a shotgun had been pointed in his direction, but his reflexes did not fail and his aim was unerring. Even as the shotgun roared, Longarm was throwing himself sideways and emptying his six-gun. He didn't stop pulling the trigger until York was dead on his feet and splayed across the bartop as if crucified by bullets.

Longarm saw a movement out of the corner of his eye near the front door and yelled, "John, the bartender!"

The sheriff pivoted and fired, but not before a bullet whistled past his face. The back bar mirror exploded into a silver shower. The bartender slapped at his forehead as if he'd been stung by a bee. His eyes rolled upward and he collapsed.

Longarm turned to see the girl and the bear disappear into a back room. To hell with them, he thought, reloading his six-gun and assessing the damage.

"I'm going after them," Sheriff Matheson said, looking very much like he wanted Longarm to help.

"I wouldn't bother," Longarm said, punching fresh bullets into his gun. "I don't see how we could have proved the bear crossed state lines anyway. And besides, he *did* look like he was having fun."

"But . . ."

Longarm found a cigar and lit it, relieved to see that his hands were steady. "John," he said, "you were as good as dead under York's threat. There wasn't any choice but to force this showdown. York chose to go down fighting rather than risk prison. The others made the same choice. It's done."

"And you think I ought to just let the girl and the bear go?"

"Yeah," Longarm said, nodding his head. "I do. Any judge or jury I ever saw would laugh you right out of court on that cruelty thing."

"Oh."

Longarm reholstered his Colt and went around behind the bar to find York's private blended whiskey and fancy crystal drinking glasses. A moment later, he and Sheriff

Matheson were enjoying the finest whiskey in Wyoming.

"To long life," Sheriff Matheson said, raising his drink in a toast.

"And to me finding Frenchy and the Perry girls."

"Yeah, that too."

Longarm and the sheriff drank the entire bottle, and before it was empty the customers slowly returned, some out of morbid curiosity, others because it was time for the girl and the bear to dance again.

But the show was over for the night. The next morning, Longarm saw the dancing partners standing at the train depot. The girl was arguing with Seamus Malloy as to whether the bear was entitled to ride with the passengers or in the cattle car.

The Wild Goose Saloon shootout was all anyone talked about for two days, and then the excitement died down and things got back to normal in Cheyenne. It was about then that Longarm, who had tirelessly interviewed dozens of people about Frenchy, finally got a break from a most unexpected source, a cowboy who heard him questioning someone else on the street.

"My name is Cyrus Painter. I just rode over from Laramie to see that dancin' bear and the girl it wanted to poke. But I think I seen them three you're a 'huntin', Deputy."

"Where?"

"They was on horses moving fast through the Laramie Mountains. When they saw me, they ducked into some trees. I thought that was strange, them being so sneaky as to hide and not greet a fella friendly. I could see that the women had hair the color of gold and tits the size of melons. I was disappointed not to get a closer look, but I wanted to see the dancin' bear so I kept ridin'."

"Describe the man."

"I wasn't looking at him! It was the wimmen that would catch your eye and make your mouth water. The man, he wasn't anything special."

"How was he dressed? What color was his hair? What kind of horses were they riding?"

"Whoa up there, Deputy! They was all riding bay horses. The man was dark with a mustache. The women were dressed in men's clothes, but they'd have had to be riding in a tent to hide their figures, and their pretty hair was pokin' out from under their hats."

"That's them," Longarm said with satisfaction. He spent the next few minutes probing for more details but getting almost no additional information.

"Here," he said, digging a ten-dollar bill out of his pants and giving it to Cyrus Painter. "You earned it and more."

"Then give me more," Painter said with a wink.

But Longarm didn't hear the man because he was already heading for the Union Pacific train depot. The way he figured it, Frenchy and his women would intercept the train further west and ride it maybe all the way to California. And if Longarm's luck was finally changing, perhaps he would be on that train when Frenchy, Loretta, and Sophie bought their tickets. If so, he'd give them a welcome they would not soon forget.

Chapter 8

Frenchy had a big problem. Actually, he had two big problems and their names were Loretta and Sophie. Since fleeing Denver, the two sisters had done nothing but bicker and fight. All day long they argued and curried his favor. If he complimented Loretta on her hair, then Sophie would pout. If he said something nice about Sophie, Loretta would fly into a jealous rage. If he said nothing about either one, that was interpreted as being ungrateful for sparing him from the hangman's noose.

Frenchy felt guilty. He didn't really even like the Perry sisters. True, they were attractive in a rough, sort of Amazon way. Tall, stately, and with the bodies of Greek goddesses, they turned heads and made men think lusty thoughts. But in truth, Loretta was a carpish woman with awful table manners and personal hygiene, while Sophie was coarse and prone to dominate and intimidate men. One of her favorite little tricks was to goose Frenchy in public so hard that he squealed with pain. This caused both sisters to laugh uproariously while Frenchy burned with humiliation.

So what was Frenchy to do? He did, after all, owe the sisters his life. They had rescued him from the hangman's rope for no other reason than that they loved and desired him despite their delight in also humiliating him. But they made his life unbearable. He could scarcely get a word in when the pair began to argue, and when they began to screech like mountain lions, Frenchy wanted nothing more than to escape.

"Frenchy," Loretta said, "you seem very quiet today. Is something wrong?"

"No, nothing is wrong," he said from the back of his horse.

"We will be in Laramie by this evening. Can we get a hotel room with a *big* bed?" Sophie gushed.

"I think that would be very unwise. We should skirt Laramie and keep riding. I'm afraid that Longarm and other federal lawmen will be riding the rails in the hope of catching us."

"Oh, Frenchy!" Loretta cried. "We're been riding and sleeping in the dirt for over a week! We stink and we need to get a hot bath. We're almost out of food too!"

"She's right," Sophie said. "For once, Loretta is right. We've got to stop in Laramie. We're out of money and—"

"If we're out of money, what good is it to stop in a big town?" Frenchy asked.

"There's money to be made in towns! Easy money."

"For you ladies, perhaps," Frenchy said. "But—"

"Our money is your money, darlin'," Loretta said with a smile. "You can be our . . . our manager from now on."

"Well, hump me with a billy goat!" Sophie exclaimed. "Sophie is finally right. You would make a hell of a good manager."

Frenchy was not sure what these girls meant by the term, but he was afraid that it meant he was to be their pimp. That role was one that he did not find the least bit appealing.

73

"Manager for what?"

"We got talents you ain't seen yet," Loretta assured him. "We can sing and dance."

"Is that right?"

"That's right," Loretta said. "I can pick a few chords on the guitar and Sophie can play more than one kind of mouth organ."

"Shut up!" Sophie said when Loretta began to chortle. "I can play a few chords myself. If we had us some guitars, you'd see how good we really are, Frenchy."

"I'm sure that I would," he said wearily. "But right now our main concern ought to be in putting as much distance between ourselves and Colorado as possible."

"So where *are* we going exactly?"

"I have friends," he said vaguely. "Friends that will hide us until the federal lawmen give up the chase. But that might take quite some time, girls. After all, you *murdered* that federal officer of the Denver court."

"That wasn't planned," Loretta confessed. "The fool went after his gun and there just wasn't any choice."

Frenchy sighed. "I sure hope that you didn't also kill Longarm and Marshal Vail. If you did, the authorities will never give up until they find us."

"Fuck 'em," Sophie said, waving her hand with feigned indifference. "We can change our appearances and find a new place to live where we won't ever be found."

That evening, they saw the lights of Laramie and followed the train tracks to the edge of the railroad town. It was not nearly as big as Cheyenne, but was agreeably situated at the western slopes of the Laramie Mountains.

"I'm hungry!" Loretta complained.

"I'm thirsty," Sophie said. "Next time we travel, we're going to make sure we have enough whiskey."

Frenchy scowled. "Girls," he said, "I wish that you

74

would reconsider stopping here, and continue west on horseback at least as far as Rawlins or even Rock Springs."

"Why, that's more than a hundred miles!" Loretta cried. "If you think my ass is going to put up with riding that far, you're in for another think. Come on, Frenchy! Aren't you ready for some fun?"

"I am, but we're running a big risk stopping here. I tell you, the feds will be swarming after us."

"We'll just stay the night," Loretta assured him. "And in the morning, we'll either ride out or take the train, if there is one passing through going west."

Frenchy could see that there was little point in arguing. So he led the way along the tracks, and when they arrived at the edge of town and a livery, he reined his horse in and hailed the liveryman.

"What the hell do you people want at this hour!" a voice from inside the big barn shouted in anger. "Come back tomorrow. I'm tired and trying to sleep."

"We need to board our horses," Frenchy said.

There were curses, followed by a wait. Then a heavyset man without shoes and dressed in big baggy overalls appeared. He was dirty and unshaven, smelling of horse. "I don't know why you people can't . . ."

Whatever he was about to say was forgotten when he raised his lantern and realized that Loretta and Sophie were women of unusual proportions.

"Well, now," he said, brushing straw from his coveralls and grinning wickedly. "What do we have here?"

"We need to know when the next westbound train is coming through."

"Two days from this morning," the liveryman said, eyes jumping from Loretta to Sophie. "You need them horses put up until then."

"We want to sell 'em," Sophie announced.

"Now wait a minute," Frenchy protested. "We agreed to leave Laramie tomorrow—one way or another."

"My butt is raw!" Sophie complained. Her eyes drifted to the liveryman. "Hey, big boy, you got any liniment?"

The liveryman gulped and licked his lips. "I sure do! Step on down and we'll have a look-see."

"Now wait just a minute," Frenchy said, dismounting. "If there is any applying of liniment, I'll do it!"

"Unless our friend would like to pay for the pleasure," Sophie said with a bold smile at the liveryman.

The liveryman yanked a dirty handkerchief out of his pocket and mopped his perspiring face. "I'd pay, all right. But how about me putting these horses up for the night in trade?"

Loretta dismounted and handed her reins to Frenchy. "We need some money to eat," she purred, swaying up to the liveryman. "So how about both of us girls for five dollars and board for the horses."

"You got it!" the liveryman whispered.

Frenchy thought he really ought to protest. It was a matter of honor. These women were traveling with him and he somehow ought to provide for them. But how? He hadn't anything of real value. Certainly nothing that he could spare to trade for money or hay and a stall.

No matter. Even as he tried to think of something to trade for services or cash, Loretta and Sophie took the liveryman's arms, turned him around, and led the way back inside the barn. Frenchy followed leading their exhausted and hungry horses. While he unsaddled, watered, and fed them, Sophie and Loretta made the liveryman's dreams come true in an empty stall filled with fresh straw. Frenchy could hear the girls whispering and the man groaning with pleasure. Frenchy knew that the Perry girls were winding the man's stem like a cheap pocket watch. When they finished winding, the liveryman began to howl.

Frenchy sighed and finished with the horses. By the time he had dusted off his clothes and gone outside, the girls were through and joined him with cash in hand.

"We got three dollars each," Loretta proudly announced.

"And earned it," Sophie replied, whacking straw from her hair. "He was a real pig. You hear him grunting like a pig, Frenchy, darling?"

Frenchy had heard. He was uncomfortable and annoyed that the Perry girls had given themselves so freely even though he had no illusions as to their character or talents. It was just that . . . well, he had wanted to protect and take care of them in repayment for saving his life. And now, it seemed, they were supporting him and not the other way around.

As they marched up the street, more than a few eyes were turned. At the first saloon, Sophie didn't wait for an invitation but pushed through the batwing doors and went inside.

"To hell with her," Loretta said, hugging Frenchy's arm. "Let's go get a hotel room and a bath, then let's screw for a while."

"I thought you were hungry."

"I am, but . . ."

"Then let's go inside, get Sophie, and find a cafe that is still open," Frenchy said. "I'm tired, dirty, and hungry myself."

"Why are you acting so mean?"

"I . . . I'm sorry."

Loretta hugged him. "Sophie can handle herself. Let's find that room."

"No," Frenchy said, "we've got to stick together until

we are in no danger of being captured by the feds."

Frenchy pulled free of Loretta and entered the dim saloon. It was a disreputable-looking establishment with dirty sawdust on the floor and a wide plank stretched across whiskey barrels instead of a real bar. There were about ten tough, suspicious-looking patrons whose full attention was on Sophie until they also saw Loretta.

"Well, I'll be go to hell," one big man said, grinning broadly. "There's *two* of the handsome bitches!"

His friends nodded.

"One looks as good as the other," the big man said. "Which of you girls wants to pleasure Big Jim first?"

"Go play with yourself," Loretta snapped, heading for the bar.

Jim flushed with anger and grabbed Loretta by the upper arm. "Honey," he said, whipping her around. "I like women with spirit so I'll take you first."

"Let go of her," Frenchy said quietly. "Those are my girls. Leave them alone."

"We can take care of ourselves," Sophie said, tossing down a glass of whiskey.

Jim backhanded Sophie. The crack of flesh against flesh made a loud, popping sound. Sophie squealed with pain and Loretta jumped at the man, fingernails digging into his cheeks and just missing the eyes.

Jim howled and smashed Loretta backward. He touched his cheek, saw the blood, and drew his knife. "Bitch, I'm gonna cut your pretty face for that!"

Frenchy's own knife was in his fist and he jumped forward to shield Loretta. "Better think again, Big Jim. Better apologize to the ladies while you still can."

"I apologize to no one! Especially whores!"

Frenchy's knife blade flashed in the lantern's light. Big Jim cried out in pain and staggered backward as a line of blood welled up from a wicked wound across his chest.

"Apologize!"

"Never!"

Big Jim lunged for Frenchy, but the quicker man easily jumped aside and his blade flashed a second time, opening up another deep gash across Jim's side. The big man turned, bent and waxen in the light.

He looked to his friends. "Someone shoot him!"

Frenchy drew his own gun and pointed it toward the crowd. "Anyone else want some of this action, step forward!"

No one moved. Frenchy, with the gun in his left hand and his Bowie knife clenched in his right, said, "I think you had better apologize right now. The next time my blade will find your heart."

Big Jim wiped his face with his sleeve. He was panting and looked unsteady on his feet. Blood was pouring from his chest and his side. His broad shoulders slumped in defeat as he turned to Loretta and Sophie.

"I . . . I apologize," he whispered, his knife slipping to the floor as he looked away.

"Louder!" Frenchy demanded.

Big Jim threw back his head. "I apologize!"

Frenchy holstered his six-gun and sheathed his knife. He went over to the bar. "Three bottles of your best whiskey!"

"Coming up!" the bartender shouted.

Frenchy uncorked one bottle, tasted, and spit whiskey into the sawdust. "This is your best?"

"Yes, sir!"

"Never mind then." He held both arms out. Sophie snatched a pair of bottles from the plank bartop and grinned. "For the road, Frenchy, for the road."

Frenchy wished that she had not spoken his nickname,

but the damage was done and there was no help for it now. "Come along, girls," he said, leading them outside. "A meal, a bath, and then sleep."

"Wait a minute!" Loretta said as they passed outside. "You forgot to mention the screwin'!"

Frenchy hadn't forgot. He just wasn't in the mood. Not after hearing that fat, dirty pig of a liveryman carry on with these two girls. Maybe, he reasoned, he could beg off from his expected duty by feigning a headache.

Chapter 9

Frenchy awoke the next morning with a real headache. Loretta was sleeping on his right, her face turned toward him and her whiskey-fouled breath making him slightly nauseous. The morning sunlight was streaming through the window of their hotel room and it was not kind to Loretta. Up close and under the bright sunlight, Frenchy could see a web of wrinkles that he had not noticed before.

He turned to Sophie, who was snoring like a drunken mule skinner, mouth hanging open, tongue lolling. Frenchy felt his stomach roll as he inched his way up between the two women and then gingerly crabbed over the top of Sophie to reach the floor. For several minutes he cradled his head in his hands, then slowly wobbled over to his clothes.

He was physically wasted. They had all gotten drunk and the Perry girls had been insatiable last night. Frenchy was still exhausted and sore from the drunken orgy he had been forced to continue almost until dawn.

"I have to get away," he said ruefully to himself. "They are pigs and they will be caught. And if I stay with them, I will be caught too!"

Frenchy began to dress. His brain was fouled by whiskey but driven by fear. Even now, Longarm or some other federal deputy marshals might be galloping into Laramie seeking to either arrest him or gun him down for the heinous killing of that Denver courtroom bailiff.

Head throbbing, foul sweat beading across his body, Frenchy grabbed his sixgun and buckled his cartridge belt around his lean waist. In truth, he felt like a traitor for leaving the Perry sisters to almost certain capture and imprisonment, if not the gallows. He wished that he could have led them to safety because he owed them that much. But they were bound and determined to wait for the next Union Pacific train moving west, and Frenchy had a dreadful feeling that very train would bring their ruin in the form of vengeance-minded lawmen.

Frenchy placed his hat gently on his head and cast one last look at the sleeping sisters. "Good-bye," he whispered. "I am sorry to do this, but you refuse to listen to my warning and so there is nothing else that I can do."

He passed out into the hallway and steadied himself, then closed the door. A few minutes later he was outside, breathing deeply of the sweet Wyoming air and trying to clear his head. Frenchy wasted no time reaching the livery.

"I'm leaving," he informed the piggish stableman. "I need our three horses."

"Well, what about them two whores?"

"They've decided to stay a while longer in Laramie."

The fat and filthy man scratched his belly and spat a stream of tobacco to the dirt. "Now I dunno about this, mister. Them two whores rode in on two of them horses, and I sure don't like the idea of you leaving without them tellin' me is all right you take their horses."

Frenchy was in a very bad mood. "Just get the damned horses and saddle them—quick!"

The man chewed faster and spat again. "I don't believe that I will, mister. You can take your own horse if you want, but the other pair stay."

Frenchy could see that this fool was going to be difficult, even impossible, to reason with. "All right," he said, appearing to cave in to the other's truculence. "Saddle my horse."

"Cost you two bits."

"Oh, the hell with it! I'll saddle my own horse. Has he already been fed and grained this morning?"

"He sure has. And I reckon you owe me for that."

"How much?"

"Two bits."

"All right," Frenchy said before he realized that he did not have one red cent on him. "Get the horse, saddle him, and I'll pay you four bits. I just need to get out of here."

"I sure don't understand why any man would leave them two pretty whores, mister. Why, I hardly slept last night thinking about 'em. I plan to use 'em in trade for as long as they stay in Laramie."

"Fine. Just get my goddammn horse saddled!"

The liveryman scowled. "You're a touchy bastard, ain't ya?"

Frenchy didn't bother to reply. He swayed over to a nearby water trough and doused his head in the cool water, and that made him feel better. After resting for a few minutes, he went into the dim barn and when his eyes adjusted to the poor light, he walked up behind the liveryman, who was cinching his saddle down.

Frenchy drew his Colt, reversed his grip, and belted the man across the back of the skull. His horse snorted with fear but Frenchy calmed it, and then dragged the heavy liveryman into an empty stall and closed the gate so that the man would not be found until he awakened several hours later.

Frenchy had seen where the liveryman lived in a little corner of the barn. It took only a few minutes to discover where the man had hidden his stash of money. The fool had stuffed it into a couple of empty chewing tobacco pouches and stuffed them in a pair of worn-out boots. Frenchy did not bother to count the money. He could do that later and it would give him something to anticipate through the long morning ahead.

As he was about to mount his horse, Frenchy decided that it would be worth a few extra minutes to saddle the other two mounts. That way, he could relay the three horses, keeping two fresh while he rode the third. No mounted lawman would then be able to overtake him, and they would have to be mounted because Frenchy had decided that it was too dangerous to take the Union Pacific westward. Instead, he would go cross-country and chart his own escape.

Leading all three horses to the door of the livery, he peered outside and down the street. After a quick glance, Frenchy decided that no one was looking in his direction.

"So long, Laramie!" he said quietly as he mounted his horse and led the other pair out and around the barn so that it was between himself and the main street.

As much as he hated to do it, Frenchy booted his horse into a gallop. Spears of pain shot through his skull with each jolting stride of his mount, and he felt as if his arm was being jerked out of its socket in his attempt to drag along the two extra horses which had belonged to Loretta and Sophie.

Jeezus, they were going to be upset when they awoke! Frenchy did not like to even think about how angry they'd become with him for abandoning them.

Oh, well!

"Hee-yaw!" he shouted, driving his heels into his mount's flanks and urging it to greater speed.

Loretta Perry was the first to awaken four hours later. She groaned and wheezed. She opened her eyes and felt pain, so she closed them again and dozed for another quarter hour. Then she heard a loud pounding at their door.

Loretta sat bolt upright. "Frenchy!" she cried, reaching to where he should have been. When she realized that he was gone, fear and anger make her scream, "Goddammn, he's gone! Who is it!"

"It's Bert!"

"Who the hell is Bert!"

"The man who owns the livery! Your man stole my money and ran off with your horses! Let me in!"

"Wake up, damn you, Sophie! We got big troubles," Loretta screeched, jumping out of bed and stumbling toward the door stark naked.

When she yanked the door open, the liveryman's jaw dropped. "Oh, my Gawd," he said.

Loretta grabbed his arm and dragged him inside. She slammed the door behind the man and said, "Repeat what you just said!"

The man repeated the awful news and ended by saying, "I had fifty dollars stolen. I guess it's gonna take you girls six months to work that much off."

Loretta wasn't listening. She grabbed Sophie and dragged her kicking out of the bed and onto the floor. "We got to get dressed! Frenchy ran out on us!"

"No!"

"It's true. He took our horses and ran!"

"Why that rotten, ungrateful sonofabitch!" Sophie cried, grabbing her clothes.

"Now wait a minute," the liveryman said. "I'm out fifty dollars and a broken skull. I mean to have this made right. You girls ain't going nowheres but back to bed with me!"

Loretta turned toward her sister and winked.

"All right," Sophie said, "come on, big boy!"

The liveryman grinned. "That's more like it!"

"Shuck 'em, big boy, and come to Mama!"

As soon as the man's gun was hanging on the bedpost and his pants were around his ankles, Loretta grabbed the big ceramic water basin off their bureau and smashed it to smithereens across the back of the man's already bloody scalp. He collapsed with a groan.

"What are we going to do now!" Sophie cried.

Loretta thought a minute. She dimly recalled how Frenchy had argued the night before that they could not risk riding the train west but had to play it safe and ride away from the Union Pacific lines. Frenchy had wanted to head directly southwest across the northern corner of Colorado into Utah.

"Loretta?"

"Finish dressing," she said. "This pig has a whole stable full of horses, doesn't he?"

"Yeah, but horse stealing is—"

"A hanging offense. And just what do you think killing that bailiff in Denver will get us if we are caught?"

"I see what you mean. But I don't know if my head and my sore ass can stand a saddle today."

"Better an aching head and sore ass than a rope-stretched neck," Loretta said, stuffing the liveryman's gun under her dress and removing a watch and a few dollars from his pockets. "Let's go!"

Twenty minutes later, they were leading four horses out around behind the barn and climbing into their saddles.

"I think I'm going to get sick," Sophie confessed, looking slightly greenish.

"Better do it on the run," Loretta said coldly. "Because with or without you, I'm going to catch and castrate that Frenchy."

"Castrate him?"

"That's right. *No* man runs out on Loretta Perry!"

Sophie didn't say anything as she booted her horse into a gallop after her sister. But she couldn't help but think that castrating Frenchy Lemond would be a terrible waste.

Chapter 10

Longarm was cautiously optimistic about his chances of snaring Frenchy Lemond and the murdering Perry girls when he arrived in Laramie. And so, when the train rolled down from the mountains into that Wyoming railroad town, Longarm wasted no time in disembarking and paying a visit to the nearest hotels. In less than fifteen minutes, he was standing before the desk of the Laramie Hotel.

"Them three skipped out of town without paying their bill," the man said gruffly. "But I guess I was damned lucky—poor Bert Waynesmith down at the livery was the one that really got shafted."

"What happened to him?"

"Why, them three took their own horses without paying and stole a passel of his boarders' horses, along with all his savings he had hid in a couple of tobacco pouches. Bert said he lost two thousand dollars!"

"Only a fool would hide that much money in tobacco pouches. Why didn't he deposit it in a bank?"

"Well, Bert, he don't trust anybody. Anyway, he's feelin' mighty low. What with his cash losses and four stolen horses to pay for, he's about ready to shoot hisself."

"Didn't anyone go after them?"

"Sure! Yesterday there was a bunch went lookin', but the roads are chewed up by horse tracks and wagon wheels. Nobody could come to an agreement as to where them three might have gone."

Longarm shook his head. "I'm a deputy United States marshal and I'm after them. I was hoping to come upon them at the train station."

"Well I guess that means we're all disappointed then, ain't we," the hotel clerk said snippishly.

Longarm ignored the man's poor manners and said, "Where can I find Bert?"

"His stable is right at the east end of town. Big, ugly barn that looks like it'd come down in a stiff breeze. He'll be there if he ain't up and put hisself out of his own misery."

"He'd do that?"

"I don't know," the hotel clerk said, shaking his head. "Bert is pretty upset."

"I'd better go see him right now." Longarm started to turn and leave.

"Say, Deputy?"

"Yeah?"

"What happened to your eye? Some fella put a thumb in and gouge it out?"

"Not exactly," Longarm said.

"Was it one of them pretty whores that did it?"

"In a way."

"Them two were poison," the clerk said. "Did they scratch it out?"

Longarm didn't feel like explaining, and left. He had no trouble finding Bert. The man was sitting on an empty horseshoe nail keg in front of his barn, chin resting on his upturned palm, his smudged and unshaven face bleak.

"You've got to be Bert Waynesmith," Longarm said.

"What's it to you?" the liveryman growled.

Longarm flashed his badge and Bert's scowl vanished. The man said, "You after them whores and that other fella?"

"That's right."

"They took four of my clients' horses and two thousand dollars of my money. You catch 'em, I want everything back."

"I'll see what I can do," Longarm said, glancing into the barn and thinking that Bert's entire operation wasn't worth two thousand dollars. "I understand that you lost their tracks?"

"That's right," Bert said. He waved absently in a circle. "Hell, there's so many ranches and cowboys around this part of the country that we found tracks heading in all directions."

"And you didn't compare them with the ones that were stolen?"

Bert's brow knitted. "What do you mean?"

"I mean that I'd like to see where all those horses were kept."

"Why?"

"Because it's my understanding that they took seven horses, including four stolen. That's twenty-eight feet."

"So?"

"So there is bound to be one or two of them with some kind of distinguishing mark."

Bert heaved a sigh and came to his feet. "I don't know how you could do it, but follow along and I'll show you where all them horses were stabled inside. I had a bunch more penned in the corral out back. Guess that I'm damned lucky they didn't take them too."

Longarm said nothing as the man showed him the empty stalls where the horses had been kept. He was disappointed to see that the stalls were covered with straw and there was no chance of reading tracks. However, in the dirt between the empty stalls and the barn door there were many distinct hoofmarks.

"Any other horses been inside since the stolen horses?"

"No."

"Good. Help me throw open these doors wide so I can get some light in here."

Bert was big and strong. The doors sagged and had probably not been fully opened in years, but together he and Longarm managed to get them open wide. The sunlight poured inside, and Longarm went down on his hands and knees and began a careful examination of the tracks. He had a small notebook and pencil in his shirt pocket, and twice he traced a hoofprint onto the paper, taking notes as well.

Bert watched with interest. "I never seen the likes of you," he said when Longarm finally completed his investigation, consulted his notes, and seemed satisfied. "Them little pictures going to lead you to Frenchy and them bitches?"

"I hope so."

"I doubt it."

"Bert, I'd like to rent a horse, maybe even a pair."

"Cost you a dollar a horse a day."

"Fine. That's about what I'll charge to return each of your horses."

"Now wait a minute! It's your damned job to return stolen horses!"

"I'm after the man and the woman. *That's* my job. The horses are an afterthought as far as I'm concerned."

"All right," Bert finally groused. "You can borrow one horse for free. But if you lose him or he gets shot, I'll expect fifty dollars for him and the saddle, bridle, and blanket."

"Fair enough," Longarm said, "if the horse is a good one. But he's got to be fast, strong of limb and lungs, shod, and have plenty of endurance."

"You don't want much, do you?"

"Look at it this way," Longarm said. "They've got relay horses. Now, if you give me an animal that's slow or has a tendency to quit in the mountains or go lame, what do you think the chances are that I'll overtake them three and return your cash and your horses?"

"Damn slim."

"Damn right."

Bert led Longarm back around behind the barn to a large pole corral where about twenty horses were penned. "Take your pick."

Longarm draped his saddlebags across the top rail and entered the corral. He didn't flatter himself into thinking he was an expert horseman, but he knew the good from the bad. And most of these horses were bad. In fact, he'd never seen a worse collection of culls and misfits.

"Where the hell did you get this poor bunch?"

"They're Indian ponies mostly. I buy 'em cheap. Sometimes a bronc buster will come in and take a few and turn 'em into pretty fair saddle horses."

"Well, I'm not a bronc buster."

"What do you think of that paint gelding?"

"He's crooked in front legs. Narrow-chested too."

"Then how about that palomino?"

"Jug-headed and too stiff in the pasterns."

"Hell," Bert said, "you got a good eye but you're damn fussy. Choose one. They're all that I got except for two in a little pen around the other side of this barn that I keep for my best customers."

"Let's have a look at 'em," Longarm said. "I sure don't think I'll catch anyone on one of these sorry plugs."

Bert wasn't pleased but Longarm wasn't either—until he saw the handsome pair of buckskin geldings.

"I'll take them both."

"Now wait a minute!"

Longarm peeled off a hundred dollars. "If anything happens to them, you're paid. If not, I'll bring them back and you can keep half the money for the rental. Does that sound fair?"

"Sure, but like I said, I got a few good customers. Men who rent them buckskins regular. They're not going to be happy about this."

"And neither will I if you don't get the buckskins saddled so that I can start chasing after those killers and horse thieves."

Grumbling, Bert took Longarm's money and pocketed it. A half hour later he had one of the buckskins saddled and the other haltered.

Bert stepped back as Longarm mounted. He scratched his belly and said, "Did them women really murder someone?"

"Yes, they did. A bailiff in Denver."

"What about the fella that was with them?"

"He's been sentenced to hang," Longarm said.

"He killed men too?"

"Three of them over wives and lovers."

"Jeezus," Bert whispered. "And he let me screw them two whores in an empty stall! I'm lucky that I didn't get shot or killed!"

"That's right," Longarm said. "You're lucky that you only lost four horses and a couple hundred dollars."

"I guess I am. And . . . now wait a minute! I lost a couple of thousand!"

"No, you didn't," Longarm said. "And you just admitted it."

Bert Waynesmith flushed with either anger or embarrassment. "Well, maybe I did stretch the money thing a little, but those were four damn good horses."

"One of them toes out real bad and another has a badly worn and twisted shoe. The kind that you'd spot in a minute if you were looking for it."

Bert nodded. "I guess that's why you're a United States federal officer and I'm running a half-assed livery about to collapse."

Longarm didn't agree or disagree. With a nod of his chin, he mounted one buckskin. "Have you any idea at all which direction that bunch lit out in?"

"Nope. And I'm afraid we messed up the ground real bad looking for sign."

"I think they went west."

Longarm rode away off to the nearest general store, where he would buy a box of rifle shells, food, blankets, and a few other odds and ends to make life a little more comfortable on what he was sure would be a long, long trail. Once he had provisioned himself, Longarm galloped about two miles west following the Union Pacific railroad tracks, and then he cut south. Bert had called it right when he said that the ground was scarred with hundreds of hoofprints, but Longarm knew that would change after he put a few more miles between himself and Laramie. After he got beyond the range of the Sunday riders and families out for a day's outing.

Early that evening, just as sunset was firing the land crimson and gilding the edges of the clouds, Longarm found the Colorado fugitives' trail. He dismounted, retrieved his notes and sketches from his shirt pocket, and carefully placed them beside the tracks. In less than five minutes, he had his hoofprint match, and when he stood up, his eyes followed the trail southwest into the northwestern corner of Colorado. Into the high desert and mountain country.

Longarm carefully folded his papers and remounted. The buckskin geldings were still fresh and eager so he rode until dark, and then he stopped and made camp.

That night, as he stared into the fire and listened to the coyote's lonesome howl, Longarm spent a lot of time thinking about Frenchy Lemond and the Perry girls. He remembered again how Frenchy had risked his own life to save the very man who was bound to see him brought to justice. It was a mystery to Longarm how a man could be both a hero and a murderer.

Women. They were the Frenchman's nemesis. Once, Frenchy had admitted that the first time he'd gotten into real trouble was when he was fifteen years old and the young wife of a Santa Fe sheriff had seduced him. A few days later, in a fit of remorse, she had confessed her sin to her jealous husband.

The sheriff had arrested Frenchy and beaten him to within an inch of his life. He'd tormented Frenchy and made his life a living hell, until Frenchy had feigned unconsciousness and then caught the sheriff off guard and knocked him senseless. He'd run south to Mexico and lived in exile for five years. It hadn't been all that bad a life because the señoritas were hot and pretty, and Frenchy had quickly discovered that women found him irresistible.

But then, he'd gotten involved with another married woman and had fought her husband with a knife. Frenchy still carried the terrible scars of that bloody encounter.

But he'd won and the jealous Mexican had died. On the run from the dead Mexican's large and vengeance-minded family, Frenchy had recrossed the border into Texas, where women troubles continued to be his downfall.

Longarm recalled Frenchy saying, "I love women! But they're bad for me. I'm like a man who can't leave the whiskey alone until it kills him. That's the way that I am. Drunk on women. Short ones, tall ones, fat ones, and skinny ones. I love them all."

"Then maybe," Longarm had commented, "you ought to confine your lovin' to the ones that aren't already married or betrothed."

To which Frenchy had barked a laugh and replied, "They're damned hard to tell apart if they slip off their rings and things."

Longarm had chuckled a little at the time, but he guessed that Frenchy had a good point. If a pretty woman was going to cheat on her husband or her lover, you weren't likely to know about it until it was too late.

Longarm fell asleep early and slept until the first light of dawn. Then, taking his time, he brewed a little strong coffee in his new pot and fried some salt pork in his new skillet. He used his knife to eat the tasty pork. Twenty minutes later, he was on the buckskin that he'd led the day before and following the trail down toward Colorado.

Late the following afternoon, he came to a small settlement. It wasn't much, just a mining town that had failed and been abandoned except for a few stubborn souls.

"Howdy," Longarm said to the first man that he saw, an old fella who was propped up in a wooden chair tilted against a boarded-up assayer's office.

"Howdy," the old fella said, thumbing a floppy gray hat up so that he could study Longarm. "You got some nice horses there, stranger."

"Thanks. I'm looking for a man with dark hair and a waxed mustache. He was leading two horses and might have come through here a couple days ago. He was with two pretty blond gals. They were also ponying extra horses."

"Yep," the old man said. "I seen 'em. Getting to be damned crowded in this part of the country. Why you looking for them?"

"I'm a federal officer of the law," Longarm said, showing the man his badge before returning it to his pocket.

"Bet you're wantin' to catch them fast wimmen more than that fella they was after to kill."

"To what?" Longarm asked, surprised.

"To kill." The old man grinned. "Them wimmen rode in after that fella was gone. They asked me if I'd seen him and I asked 'em why they asked. They told me that the fella had shot their husbands."

"They did?"

"That's right," the old man said. "Did they lie?"

"Yeah."

"Well, they said that they were on his trail and fixin' to kill him. To avenge the deaths of their menfolks. That's just how they put it too."

Longarm dismounted. It was noon and he had no appetite for more salt pork. "So where were they all heading?"

"The fella was in kind of a hurry. You could see that he'd been running his horses hard. I don't think them wimmen will ever catch him. He could ride better'n either one of them wimmen."

"Were they heading south or west?"

"Beats the hell out of me," the old man said, leaning over to spit a stream of tobacco juice, which arched over the boardwalk and soaked into the street.

He squinted at Longarm and said, "If you're huntin' 'em and you're really a fed, I guess you know enough about trackin' to follow their trail."

"Yeah," Longarm said, "I guess I do." He looked around. "Looks like the town has about closed down for good. Any place where a man can eat and spend the night?"

"There's a saloon just up the street. Looks closed but it ain't. They'll cook you up a supper of fish and beans for two bits. Beer is green but only a nickel."

"What about my horses?"

"I'll put them up for two bits each, same as I put up them other horses." The old man chuckled. "You won't believe what them women wanted to do in exchange for their board and feed bill."

"I can imagine," Longarm said. "There's a fella over in Laramie took them up on the offer and he's damned sorry."

"They looked like they could really perk up a man's pisser."

"Oh, they could, all right. But they have a way of turning around and robbing you and maybe bashing in your skull for good measure."

The old man's eyes widened. "Well, then, I'm glad I wasn't a couple of years younger or I might just have tried on them yeller-haired wimmen!"

"Yeah," Longarm said, handing his reins to the old man before he wearily plodded down the street to find a bite to eat and a few green beers to wash down his supper.

Chapter 11

When Frenchy rode into the Mormon logging settlement
of Purity, Utah, he was out of money and food. His horses
were exhausted and one of them had gone lame. There was
a haunted, wary look in his eyes. A hundred times each
day Frenchy had found himself glancing back over his
shoulder expecting to see either the Perry girls or a federal
lawman. Frenchy was not overly fond of Mormons, but he
admired them for their hard work and sobriety. They were
a close-knit and clannish people and he did not expect that
he would have much luck recouping his fortunes in Purity.

"Afternoon," he said to the stern-faced blacksmith as
he reined his horse to a standstill.

The blacksmith didn't return the greeting but kept
on working. He was short, barrel-chested, and round-
shouldered with humped muscle. In his early forties, the
blacksmith was still an imposing specimen of manhood
with a heavy brow and a thick stump of neck. His thighs
were as thick as whiskey kegs and he probably weighed
about 220 pounds, all of it bone and muscle.

Someone had lately given the blacksmith the worst
haircut that Frenchy had ever seen inflicted on a white
man. It was like they'd used a pair of scissors and just

chopped off big hunks of hair until the scissor blades broke. Hell, Frenchy realized, maybe the haircut had been administered by one of the poor man's wives using a dull knife. In a town like Denver or Cheyenne or even Santa Fe, a man with such a sorry haircut would have been made a laughingstock. But up here in these Utah mountains, probably no one noticed or cared.

The blacksmith paused with his hammer raised over his anvil, a horseshoe in the grip of his tongs. He nodded to Frenchy without comment.

Realizing that he was not going to receive a friendly greeting, Frenchy said, "My horses are thirsty. Mind if I water 'em in your trough?"

"Suit yourself."

"Much obliged," Frenchy said, stiffly dismounting.

He watered his three horses and surveyed the town. It probably had a population of five or six hundred, which was big for a Wasatch Mormon community.

"Nice town," Frenchy said. "Real nice town."

The blacksmith scowled. He began to hammer on the horseshoe and work his forge. When Frenchy's horses had their fill of water and were hungrily eyeing a nearby stack of hay, Frenchy made a big show of picking up the lame horse's hoof.

"This horse of mine threw a shoe yesterday. He's already half lamed. Too nice a horse to let go like this, but I'm a little short of money right now."

The blacksmith stopped hammering, but instead of offering to shoe the animal he said, "I'll give you ten dollars for that lame horse."

"Ten dollars! Why, he's worth thirty lame! Take a look at his foot. Once he's shod again, he'll be sound."

Instead of acting on Frenchy's offer, the blacksmith resumed working at his forge. Frenchy swore under his breath. This man was going to be tough to strike any kind of a fair deal with, that was for sure. Frenchy also knew that his own circumstances were obviously desperate and that anyone would realize he was not in a strong bargaining position. The blacksmith would see that the horse had to be shod or it might sustain permanent hoof damage. And since he was the only blacksmith in Purity, he was going to make a killing.

"How much would you charge to tack a rough old shoe on this horse?" Frenchy asked. "Wouldn't even have to be a new one as long as it still had a few miles on it."

"Three dollars."

"Three dollars! That's robbery!"

"Suit yourself." The blacksmith looked at Frenchy without pity. "Your horse is lame. It'll be bear meat long before you get to Salt Lake City."

Frenchy reached into his pockets and pulled them inside out. "As you can plainly see, I'm dead broke. I haven't eaten in two days, my horses are starved down to nothing, and I need this horse shod. Hell, they all need to be shod!"

The blacksmith nodded, but without sympathy.

Frenchy wanted to walk up and punch the man in the face, but that would have been a mistake. The blacksmith was far too strong and Frenchy knew that he was not equal to him in a stand-up fist fight.

"Well how about me working in trade for a couple of meals for myself and my horses—and a fresh shoeing for all three horses?"

The blacksmith looked at him for a moment, then said, "Show me your hands."

"Huh?"

"Show me your hands!"

Frenchy raised them up, not understanding. The powerful blacksmith waddled over and grabbed his hands. He grunted, "Softer than a woman's, that's for durn sure."

"But stronger." Frenchy could see that the blacksmith's hands were heavily calloused and as tough as rawhide.

"You can't work," the Mormon said with contempt.

Frenchy bristled. "Sure I can work! Why . . . why I can build and dig and load wagons. If need be, I can do a lot of things. And right now, I have to."

When the blacksmith didn't say anything, Frenchy turned his back on the man. "I'll find someone else in this town that needs help. And when I do, I'll get me the three dollars and you'll put a complete set of shoes on that lame horse for three dollars!"

The blacksmith waited until Frenchy had a boot in his stirrup before he said, "I got a half mile of fence post to cut and set in the ground. You want to do them?"

"For a set of horseshoes and a few meals? Hell, no! I'm in bad shape, that's plain to see. But I'm not in *that* bad shape."

"I'll shoe all three of your horses, feed and shelter you and them, and give you . . . five dollars."

"For erecting a half mile of fence posts? Why, you must be crazy! That'd take a month at least."

He finished mounting and started to ride off, but changed his mind. Twisting around in his saddle, he said, "I'll work for three days cutting and setting posts. You can keep your cash, but you got to feed me all I want and not only shoe all my horses, but grain 'em as well."

The blacksmith gazed off toward the mountains for so long that Frenchy thought the man had even forgotten he existed.

"Well?" Frenchy demanded.

The blacksmith turned back to face him. "Mister, there's an ax in my shop. Trees are up yonder. I'll hitch up a wagon. You'll cut and set twenty a day or

102

you'll ride barefooted horses down from these mountains."

Frenchy did not know how hard it would be to cut and trim that many posts and set them deep enough in the ground to support a couple strands of barbed wire, but he figured that it would be a ball-buster. These Mormons were ants for work and few could match their herculean output.

"I'll give it my best," he said. "But right now, I've got to get something to eat."

The blacksmith wasn't pleased. No doubt he'd not expected to feed Frenchy until dark, and then only after seeing how hard he'd worked during the long afternoon. But Frenchy looked so weak and exhausted that the Mormon said. "My house is over yonder. The women will feed you good. Eat quick and come back. The ax will be sharp and the wagon ready."

"I will," Frenchy promised.

He started to leave, but the blacksmith said, "Leave them horses, mister. My name is Robert Jenner. You tell my Irma I said to feed you good."

"I will do that."

Frenchy left his horses and hurried up the road to the blacksmith's big log cabin. At his approach, he saw several women of various ages and a crowd of healthy children. When they saw him coming, the children ran around behind the huge cabin and then kept peeking around the corners to watch him. Frenchy smiled at them but they didn't smile back.

Irma Jenner came out to greet him. She was a heavyset and unattractive woman just as suspicious of outsiders as her husband. When Frenchy explained the arrangement, the woman sent a boy racing up the road to the blacksmith just to confirm what had been said. A few minutes later, the boy returned and Frenchy was told to take a seat on a log.

"How hungry are you?"

"Hungry enough to eat a horse."

"You even look hungry," the woman said, her expression softening. "You look like you've ridden a long, hard trail."

"I have," Frenchy admitted, "and it isn't over."

She smiled. "We're going to feed you like a horse, Mister . . ."

"French," he said quickly. "Mr. Thomas French."

"Well, Mr. French, you eat as much as you want because my husband will make you earn it."

"I will, Mrs. Jenner. I sure will."

Food was brought to him quickly. Lots of food. There were strips of cooked beef, potatoes, corn, and fresh-baked bread layered with butter. Frenchy devoured the meal and asked for more. Mrs. Jenner sent a girl back into the cabin for another plate, and Frenchy finished that one off too. When he couldn't eat another bite, he begin to pay some attention to Jenner's wives. Most were grim-faced and they ranged from their early twenties up to Irma, who was pushing fifty. A few of the younger ones were comely, but most were not. Frenchy counted six, and there were more children than he could imagine.

"Quite a family you have, Mrs. Jenner."

"They're a joy and a blessing. Did you get enough to eat?"

"I did."

"Then I guess you'd better get to work."

"Yeah," he said with a sigh, "I guess I should at that."

Frenchy spent the rest of the afternoon chopping down small pines that grew under big pines. They were right for

104

fence posts and since they were canopied by the bigger pines, they probably would have died anyway before they ever felt the grace of sunlight.

The blacksmith came over to show him where the fence line was to run, and Frenchy set right to work with pick and shovel. The ground, as he'd expected, was hard and rocky. By sundown Frenchy's hands were blistered and he was so tired that he could barely stand.

That evening the Jenner family ate inside, but Frenchy remained outside and balanced his heaping plate on the log again. When he was stuffed and satisfied, he spread his blankets on the floor of Jenner's barn and slept like the dead.

The next day, Frenchy worked hard. Every muscle in his body rioted in protest and his hands blistered. The prettiest of Jenner's young Mormon wives took mercy and offered Frenchy a pair of leather gloves with a shy smile.

"I'm grateful," he said, meaning it.

Holly blushed. "You're not a man much accustomed to hard work, are you, sir."

"No," he confessed, "I am not."

She shrugged her shoulders and brushed a tendril of hair back from her brow. Frenchy realized that she was actually a very pretty young woman. This fact was partially hidden by her baggy, faded dress and the men's work boots that covered her feet. But with a little fixin', Holly would be quite attractive.

"Are you going through Salt Lake City?" she asked, suddenly very serious.

"Why, I dunno. I hadn't thought much farther than getting out of these mountains."

"I hope you go to Salt Lake City, Mr. French."

"Why?"

Before she could form a reply, Irma Jenner called her name and Holly whirled and raced away leaving Frenchy to wonder.

By the morning of the third day, he'd forgotten all about Holly. Frenchy's thoughts were focused on his work. Twenty fence posts a day had proven to be an impossible goal, but Frenchy just kept working as hard as he could. To hell with the twenty posts anyway! Frenchy wasn't one to worry about what he could not control, so he occupied his mind by thinking about how good it would be to leave Purity on freshly shod horses. The horses would be rested enough to carry him across this inhospitable Mormon land and into Nevada, where he hoped to lose himself from the law and become a wealthy mine owner.

But on the afternoon of the third day, just after his noon meal, Frenchy was jolted when the blacksmith said, "You've only set forty-two posts. I'll not shod your animals until you give me sixty."

"I've done my best for you!" Frenchy shouted. "Why, I've never worked harder in my life! And you're getting off cheap. You couldn't have hired an Indian for half as much as my labor has been worth."

"Sixty posts will stand before you leave, and not one less," Jenner said without blinking.

Frenchy found himself shaking with anger. He had even imagined that this man might give him a grudging thanks for working so hard for so little compensation. Instead he'd gotten this harsh command. It wasn't right.

Frenchy stood. "I'm leaving in the morning and I'll expect my three horses to be shod."

"Sixty posts in the ground," Jenner said without compromise. "And until you plant them, they'll be no horses shod by me."

Frenchy began to tremble. His hands balled at his sides and it wasn't fear that kept him from lashing out at Jenner, but instead the certain knowledge that nothing would be gained from getting into a fistfight against a stronger man. And even if, somehow, he did best the powerful blacksmith, what then? He'd still have a lame horse and two others that would soon go lame without new shoes.

"All right," he heard himself whisper. "I'll get your sixty posts cut and set. But this isn't fair."

"It was our agreement and it stands," Jenner said in a gruff voice.

Frenchy worked like a crazed man the rest of that day, but he had to go deeper into the forest for his posts and that took extra time. By nightfall he was still ten short, and he knew that it would take most of the following day to cut, trim, and set them. It seemed as if the blacksmith had gotten four instead of three days of hard work in exchange for meals and shoeing three horses. And always, there was the worry that Longarm or the Perry girls would overtake him. If they did, this Mormon settlement would never be the same. The citizens of Purity would be talking about him well into the next century.

Frenchy arose before dawn the fourth day and went to work. He set six posts by noon, and trudged over to the Jenner cabin and slumped down on the log. A few minutes later, Holly brought out his plate.

"Thanks," he growled.

"You'll be leaving next day after tomorrow, I expect?"

"Tomorrow," he said bitterly. "I've got to leave at dawn."

"Why?"

Frenchy could not imagine what the girl's reaction would be if he told her the real reason. That he was most certainly being hunted by federal lawmen, and probably also chased

107

by the Perry girls. No, Frenchy reasoned, he certainly could not tell this innocent beauty *that* tale.

"Mr. French?"

"Yes."

Holly twisted at the folds of her homespun dress. "I want to tell you something. Something important."

"I'm listening."

"Mr. French, I'm not married to Mr. Jenner."

He looked up from his plate, mouth stuffed with potatoes and beef. "You're not?"

"I was married to his young brother, Zeb. But Zeb was killed when a tree fell on him."

"I'm sorry."

"Me too." The girl toed the ground with her ugly boots. "Mr. Jenner expects I'll marry him."

"Will you?"

"Don't want to." Holly gulped. "I . . . I don't like him much."

"Then don't marry him," Frenchy said. "And if it helps to ease your conscience, I don't like Robert Jenner either."

"Would you take me away?" she blurted out.

Frenchy had been about to stuff another piece of bread into his mouth. Now his hand froze. "Take you away where?"

"To Salt Lake City. I got cousins there. They'll take care of me until I find another man of my choosing."

"I can't do that." Having Jenner and his Mormon friends also breathing down his backtrail was the very last thing that Frenchy needed in addition to all his other troubles.

"Mr. French, please help me! You've even got three sound horses."

"Yes, but . . . well, you don't know the trouble I'm in right now. It would be dangerous. Yes, that's what it

108

would be, dangerous for you to come along."

"If I stay here," Holly said, eyes glistening, voice trembling, "I'll for sure have to marry Mr. Jenner."

"Why?"

"I just will!"

Frenchy believed her. There was just too much pain and anguish in Holly's voice to be faked.

"Mr. French, it can't be more'n sixty or seventy miles down off these mountains to the Salt Lake Valley. You wouldn't even have to go into the town, just leave me to walk once we're down out of these mountains."

"I couldn't do that."

"It'd be all right!"

"I . . . well, I don't know how it would even work. Mr. Jenner would try to stop you, and then he'd probably gather a posse and come after us."

"But we'd be gone! Let's go tonight."

"I'm not sure that my horses are reshod."

"Yes they are." Holly reached out and touched his hand. "I saw Mr. Jenner shoe 'em all today. But he expects you to stay an extra day longer."

"What?" Frenchy djd not believe his ears. "Are you sure?"

"Of course. I heard him tell Irma that last night. He says, because it would take you an extra day to set them sixty posts, he would have to spend extra money feeding you and your horses. So he's going to make you work another extra day."

"The hell I will!"

"Shhh!" Holly placed her finger over her lips. "If they see you getting upset, they'll know I told you about the extra day. That's why we should leave tonight. I know the trail. But if I lit out on my own, they'd catch me sure."

"They'll catch you sure anyway if you go straight to your cousins," Frenchy said. "You might as well give up the plan."

Tears formed in her eyes. "I just don't care for Mr. Jenner! I prayed on it. I want to do the right thing, believe me."

"I believe you."

"Then will you help me to leave Purity tonight? You're my only chance."

Frenchy looked into those glistening eyes and realized he was nodding his head up and down in agreement. "All right," he heard himself whisper. "You come out to the barn and wake me. We'll steal down to the horses, saddle them, and ride out. That way we'll have at least a four- or five-hour head start down the mountain."

"Thank you, Mr. French! Thank you very, very much!"

Frenchy grinned. Ordinarily, at this point, he would have slipped his arm around the girl's slender waist and whispered sweet words in her ear, then taken advantage of her innocence and gratitude. But this time, he just couldn't. It was clear that Holly had loved her former husband and was terrified of marrying the stern and unappealing Robert Jenner. Saving her was the only gallant thing for Frenchy to do.

"It's an honor to be of assistance to a lady," he heard himself tell her as he raised and kissed the back of her hand.

Holly sighed and gulped. She kissed *his* hand, and then she rushed away leaving Frenchy to worry about the wisdom of this new promise to a pretty woman. Every time he did something like this, he got into a bad fix. But what else could he do? Leave the poor frightened girl? Of course not!

Frenchy tried to go to sleep. He thought a little about the Perry girls and how crude and coarse they were in comparison to sweet, delicate Holly. And he thought about the Mormon men of Purity. They'd band together and come after him like a swarm of yellow jackets. And God help him if he was caught because, while the Perry girls might punish him and Longarm might kill him, the men of Purity would watch him dance on the end of a rope placed around his neck by Robert Jenner himself.

Chapter 12

"Wake up, Mr. French!" the urgent voice demanded.

Frenchy opened his eyes and blinked away sleep. He could see the Mormon girl kneeling beside him, bathed in a flood of moonlight that shafted down through the barn door. Holly was dressed in a man's baggy pants and heavy woolen shirt. A slouch hat covered the top part of her face and she was carrying a leather satchel, probably holding everything she owned in the world.

Holly looked pale and frightened.

Frenchy sat up and knuckled his eyes. "What time is it?"

"About midnight," Holly replied. "One of the women was sick earlier so it kept the entire household awake."

"Uggh," Frenchy grunted, pushing himself unsteadily to his feet. "I swear that every muscle in my body is trying to pay me back for mistreating them so bad these past four days."

When Holly said nothing, Frenchy touched her arm. "Look, don't look so worried! The worst that could happen is that these Mormons would overtake us and bring you back to Purity."

"I won't marry Mr. Jenner!" Holly cried in a fit of

passion. "I don't care if they catch me and string me up by my toes, I still won't marry that man!"

Frenchy took the slight young woman into his arms. She was trembling and he held her tight. "Holly, don't worry. No one can make your marry someone that you don't love."

"Oh, yes they can."

"No matter. They won't catch us. I've got some friends in Nevada. They'll help us both. No one will find us where I'm bound. I'll take care of you, Holly."

She turned her face up to his. Her eyes were glistening with tears of relief. She whispered, "Promise?"

"Sure I promise."

"I've got money," she said in a rush. "Plenty of money to get us a new start."

"That would help. It would help a lot."

"Let's go now," she urged. "Please?"

Frenchy nodded. He had fallen asleep on a bed of straw, and now he disengaged himself from Holly, grabbed his hat, and was ready to go.

Holly proved herself to be good with horses. She knew how to saddle and bridle her own mount, and was ready to ride almost as soon as Frenchy. He watched her tie the heavy satchel onto her saddle.

"What all do you have in there?"

"Everything I own," she said. "And some food I sneaked for us to eat tomorrow morning."

"Good." Frenchy led his horse around behind the barn so that it was situated directly between himself and the Jenner house. He mounted, and looked up at the sky when he heard the sound of thunder.

"Holly, it looks to me like a summer storm is rolling in."

"I hope not. I'd be miserable riding all wet and cold."

"True, but it might wash out our tracks. They'd just assume that we are heading for Salt Lake City."

"Aren't we going there first?"

"I'm not," Frenchy said. "You can make up your own mind once we get down from these mountains."

"I'm sticking with you," she told him, moving her horse in close. "I know that you won't allow them to bring me back here to Purity."

"I would fight them first."

Holly offered him a smile that made Frenchy feel very good. After all, given the tense circumstances, it took a very brave girl to smile. Holly was the kind of girl that a man didn't mind risking his life to help.

"Let's go," he said as thunder crashed and a bolt of jagged lightning split the night sky. "Let's put some long ground between us and these folks before daylight."

They rode off through the forest that Frenchy had worked so hard in to clear for fence posts. The horses were frisky and nervous. Whenever the lightning flashed and the thunder rolled, the horses pranced with excitement. It was all that Frenchy could do to manage his own horse as well as drag along the third horse, which was also having fits.

"I almost liked these damned horses better when they were too worn down to do much more than walk," Frenchy muttered to himself as the first big, cold raindrops began to pelt him.

He twisted around in the saddle and shouted over the wind. "Holly, stay close in this forest!"

She shouted an answer that was drowned out by the thunder. When a bolt of lightning flashed, he twisted around and could see her pale but determined face. Her hat had blown away and her brown hair was streaming in the wind. Frenchy wished like anything that there was a cabin up ahead that they could hole up in during this storm.

Frenchy had no idea where a road or trail was that would lead west through the heavy forest. That became apparent when his horse suddenly came to a standstill. After swatting the stubborn beast a few times with the ends of his reins, Frenchy dismounted and stepped ahead to realize that he was standing at the edge of a steep precipice.

"Holly!" he shouted. "Do you have any idea where we can find the road leading out of these mountains?"

"I think so."

"Get down. We're going to have to lead the horses until we can find the road."

Holly dismounted and, together, they hurried along in the night. Cold, hard raindrops pelted their faces. The horses were skittish. A jagged bolt of lightning struck a lone pine tree and it ignited like a pitch torch. Frenchy heard a cry and turned to see Holly being dragged by her mount.

"Hold on!" he cried, pulling his own terrified horses after the girl.

Somehow Frenchy managed to get all three animals under control, but Holly had been injured, probably stepped on by her plunging mount. She was writhing in pain on the trail.

"What's wrong?" he yelled into the wind.

"It's my right leg! I got kicked."

Frenchy cursed. It was impossible to try and control three frightened horses and also attend to the injured girl. In an act of desperation, he grabbed Holly and swung her back up into the saddle.

"Hang on tight!" he yelled, leading the horses onward.

Somehow, with Holly shouting instructions into the

storm, they found a wagon track leading westward. But the rain was starting to come down in icy sheets and the road was turning into a gutter of mud. Frenchy lowered his head and kept slogging forward. Now and then, he would look back and see the girl hunched up in her saddle looking like a beaten child.

Frenchy's boots became so mud-caked that each stride was an effort. The storm was pounding the Wasatch Mountains, and Frenchy could hear trees explode like cannon shots as they were struck by more lightning. On and on he slogged, until at last he came to a narrow bridge that was about to be breached by a rain-gorged stream.

"I don't know if it's safe to cross!" he yelled back at the girl. "The bridge could be swept away any minute!"

"We've got to take the risk!" Holly cried.

Frenchy knew that she was right. To stop here was to give up all hope of escaping those who pursued him. And while there might be another sturdier bridge either up or down this torrent, Frenchy knew that it would take many precious hours to locate it.

"All right," he said, "hang onto that saddlehorn and say your prayers!"

The bridge was constructed of five large tree trunks laid side by side to span the narrow gorge. In normal times, the streambed below was probably little more than a creek. But this was not normal times and the bridge was clattering, each log vibrating to its own ominous rhythm like the prongs of a tuning fork.

"Come on, horses!" Frenchy yelled, bolting forward and dragging the reluctant beasts after him.

The moment the horses landed on the bridge, Frenchy could feel it begin to slip sideways. The horses could feel it too and they lunged forward, almost knocking Frenchy into the torrent. One horse's leg actually broke through between the logs as the others bounded across. Frenchy had a terrible moment of indecision as he heard Holly cry out for help and at the same time saw the trapped horse thrashing helplessly as the bridge began to separate.

"Mr. French!"

He twisted around in time to see Holly's horse vanish into the swirling dark waters. The poor animal was swept away in an instant. Frenchy turned around and raced toward the place where he'd last seen Holly.

"Holly!" he called. "Holly!"

Running hard through the darkness, he collided head-on with a pine tree and was knocked unconscious for a moment. Regaining his feet, he groggily plunged forward again and ran until he tripped over a tree root and rolled into a little clearing where Holly and her horse were waiting. The horse's head was down and both it and the girl were trembling with fear and the chills.

Holly jumped down from her mount and hobbled over to Frenchy. "Are you all right?" she whispered, hugging him as the lightning and thunder crashed across the dark heavens.

The cold rain washed away the cobwebs and Frenchy sat up. "Where are the horses! We've got to have horses!"

Holly helped Frenchy to his feet and, together, they caught her horse and then another that appeared. Mounted again, they reined about and retraced their path back to the river. The bridge was gone and so was Frenchy's third horse, the one that had thrown a shoe on the far side of Purity.

Another wicked spear of lightning shivered across the dark heavens, and Frenchy realized he'd lost his hat and that his head was pounding with pain. He touched his forehead and felt a bloody goose egg, compliments of the tree he'd blindly collided with while racing after Holly.

She dismounted and clung to him. "Let's get out of here!"

"Yeah," he said, trying to collect his thoughts. "We need to find a cabin or some kind of shelter to hole up in until this storm passes."

Both mounted again, they rode hard through the terrible storm. It wasn't until daylight that the storm passed and they found shelter. Under the overhang of a sandstone cliff they made a small fire, and huddled shivering beside it until their clothes and bodies were warm and dry again.

"Your poor head," Holly murmured.

"You should have seen the tree that I crashed into," Frenchy answered with a tired smile. "Now that was *really* banged up."

Holly giggled and laid her head on Frenchy's shoulder. "I'm so sorry we lost your third horse."

"Me too."

"I'll make it up to you," Holly promised. "I swear that I will. I have a lot of money."

"Yeah," Frenchy said, "you told me that before. Where did it come from? Your late husband?"

"No," she said, "he didn't have any cash money. Everything my husband got went back into livestock and such."

"Then . . ."

"I took it from Mr. Jenner."

Frenchy recoiled. "You stole his money!"

"No, of course not! When my husband died, Mr. Jenner sold everything my husband owned and took me into his house. I thought he was just being kind and I liked his family so I stayed. Only later did I understand that he was after my money."

"How much do you have?"

"Eight hundred dollars," Holly told him proudly. "It's a lot, isn't it?"

"It is," Frenchy said.

"You could have what you need," Holly told him, digging around in her satchel until she found the roll of bills. "Here."

"No," he said quickly. "Put it back and keep it hidden. I don't want you to flash that around. Understand?"

"Yes, but—"

"Even if we do shake the Mormons and everyone else that is following me, we could get bushwacked if anyone suspected you were carrying that much cash."

"All right." Holly pulled up her pants leg and inspected the purplish bruise on her shin. "I was afraid that it was broken."

"Thank God that it isn't," Frenchy said. "Now, if you've got some food packed, let's eat it and be on our way. Maybe this storm was the best thing that could have happened. It might have washed out our tracks as well as that log bridge. Maybe those Mormon men won't bother to come any farther."

"Mr. Jenner will. Once he discovers that my money is gone, he'll come. That's a lot of money and he'll want it back."

Frenchy scowled. "If he comes, it'll be a waste of time and horseflesh. I won't let him have your money, Holly. And I won't let him have you."

Holly beamed. She hugged him and he liked the smell of her. Taking her hand, he said, "You and me are going to make a real good pair, Holly. I have a feeling that, unlike some of the women that I've fallen in with before, you'll be good luck."

"You think so?"

"I do," he said. "Now let's have a bite to eat and get riding."

They ate quickly, and then Frenchy carried Holly to her

horse and deposited her into her saddle. She was feather-light. And in the warm mountain sunlight her hair shone like polished mahogany wood.

"You're a pretty girl, Holly. And once you learn how to fix yourself up and wear a lady's clothes, you're going to be a real beauty."

"I will?"

"You will," he promised.

Holly looked happy enough to burst. And when Frenchy climbed back into the saddle, they held hands and rode down the muddy mountain road side by side.

Chapter 13

When Longarm rode into Purity, Utah, at first glance it appeared to be a sleepy, uneventful logging town. His buckskin horses being weary, Longarm reined into the little town's one and only livery to inquire about boarding both animals. His request was met with a glare of anger and suspicion.

"You'd best ride on," an old man said. "Folks around here are pretty upset with strangers these days."

"I'm looking for two blond women and a single individual named Frenchy Lemond." Longarm then gave a brief description of the trio of fugitives. "Do you have any idea if they passed through this way?"

"And who are you to be looking for 'em?"

"I'm a United States deputy marshal," Longarm said, flashing his badge.

The old man squinted up at it, and after a moment said, "That Frenchy fella came through here. Called himself Mr. French. He spent about three days and then kidnapped one of Mr. Jenner's intended wives."

"No."

"It's the foul truth!" The old man was whittling on a piece of wood as the shavings flew faster. "And he did it after Mr. Jenner gave him a job. Not only that, but a place to sleep in his barn and the care of his three horses. I tell you, that fella was pure skunk."

"You say he took another man's intended wife?"

"That's right. And *she* stole a big wad of Mr. Jenner's money!"

"You don't say."

"I do say!" The old man shook his head. "I'm watching over this here livery right now for Mr. Jenner while him and a posse are out looking for that fella and the girl he kidnapped."

"Why, I doubt he kidnapped her," Longarm offered. "You see, women just love Frenchy. They get attached to him real quick, and then they tag along until he gets tired and leaves them someplace."

"Hmmph!" the old man grunted. "I doubt that Jenner would believe his wife left him and this town of her own free will."

"Well," Longarm said, "it doesn't much matter to me what he believes. The fact of the matter is that I do know Frenchy and he's never had to kidnap a girl in his life. They flock to him like bees to honey."

"He took her away and after convincing her to steal Mr. Jenner's money. And I tell you something else, Mr. Deputy Marshal, our boys will capture and string him up. Mark my words!"

"Much obliged for your help," Longarm said. "And what about the other two I mentioned?"

"A pair of yellow-haired sisters?"

"That's right."

"Ain't seen 'em in Purity."

This news did not surprise Longarm. He'd lost Loretta and Sophie's tracks when they'd joined a larger group of horsemen. There had been a tough decision to make at that time, and Longarm had chosen to go after Frenchy rather than the Perry girls, whom he could easily find later. Frenchy was going to be the harder one to catch. Not only was he a hell of a lot less conspicuous that the two buxom sisters, but far less predictable. Longarm was hoping to find the Perry girls in Salt Lake City. But Frenchy? Well, that man's ultimate destination was anyone's guess.

"How long ago did Frenchy and the girl leave?"

"Two days ago. Mr. Jenner was fit to be tied. He and about a half dozen of the townsmen went right after them the next morning. But there had been a storm and the goin' was pretty rough. Most likely, they ran off to Salt Lake City."

Longarm dismounted. "I'm worn out and so are my horses. I'd like the use of the barn tonight. I can bed down there and I'll pay you for some grain, hay, and any vittles you can rustle up for me."

"Let me see that badge again, mister."

Longarm retrieved it from his pocket, and the old man took it in his gnarly hands and stared at it for several minutes before handing it back. He studied Longarm and said, "You sure don't look like a lawman."

"I don't?"

"Nope. You look more like an outlaw."

"Well, I'm not," Longarm said defensively. "Now, can I put my horses up inside?"

"After you pay me two dollars you can."

Longarm paid the old man and led his horses into the barn. He heard the rumble of distant thunder, and he wondered if another storm was about to batter these high Utah mountains. Longarm hoped not. He was tired and still damp from the last rainsquall.

"What happened to your eye?" the old man asked. "Some rotten little kid throw a rock and put it out on ya?"

"No," Longarm said. He reached up and lifted the patch. He blinked at the man and replaced the patch. "You can see that I have an eye."

"It looks okay to me. Why do you wear the patch?"

"It's a long story," Longarm said. "But the eye isn't back to normal and it messes up my vision. When I remove the patch, I find that I can't shoot what I aim for."

"I see," the old man said, holding his hand out to be paid.

Longarm paid him. He looked up and down the streets of Purity. "No saloons, I suppose?"

"Nope." The old man gloated. "Not a drop of devil's rum in the whole darned town either."

Before Longarm could say anything, his stomach rumbled. "I guess you'd better go see if you can scare me up something to eat, old-timer. My stomach is about to gobble up my gizzard."

The old man didn't laugh or even grin at Longarm's poor attempt at humor. Instead, he hobbled off toward town while Longarm settled down to wait for something to eat and to consider what he would do if he overtook Frenchy Lemond only to discover that the Mormon posse had caught and hanged him first.

That evening, Longarm was visited by Mrs. Irma Jenner. "I'm sorry to bother you," she said, "but I think it's important that we talk."

"That'd be fine, Mrs. Jenner. I understand that some girl ran away with Frenchy Lemond after stealing several thousand dollars of your husband's money."

The woman looked down at her feet, and her hands fidgeted nervously. "Well, Deputy, that's what I wanted to talk to you about. You see, the money really didn't belong to my husband."

"I beg your pardon?"

"It was Holly's money," the woman said in a clipped voice. "It came from the sale of her house, cattle, and horses. My husband had graciously offered to take her into our family."

"As a wife?" Longarm asked.

The woman nodded. "She would have been happy among us, sir. In fact I thought she *was* happy. At least she seemed to be so."

"Obviously she was not," Longarm said, wondering how any woman could be happy sharing a husband with other women. Especially a young, good-looking woman.

"No," Mrs. Jenner said, "obviously not. It was a great shock to all of us when she ran off with that man. He seemed nice. He was a hard worker too. I rather liked him. But now, I understand that he is a murderer."

Longarm frowned. "Frenchy Lemond never murdered anyone. He's killed men, but always in a fair fight. Frenchy's trouble is women, and I'm afraid that he just loves them and leaves them."

"Poor Holly!"

"Yeah," Longarm said, "she didn't show very good judgment when she ran off with Frenchy. I doubt that he'll put up with her very long. He has this uncanny knack for attracting women. But he's their poison, just as they are his poison, if you know what I mean."

"I'm not sure that I do," Irma Jenner said, looking both confused and embarrassed. "But I'll take your word for it. The important thing to say is that my husband was furious when Holly ran off with her money. He'd . . . well, he'd sort of counted on it to buy some pastureland nearby. It wounded his pride a little too. I mean, everyone in Purity thought . . . well, it has just never happened up here before."

"I understand."

"Then I hope that, when you overtake Holly, you'll tell her that we don't hold it against her for leaving. And that we know she didn't steal our husband's money but only took what was rightly her own."

"I'll tell her," Longarm said. "But that doesn't explain why your menfolk went after Frenchy. I mean, he took only his own horses, and if the money belonged to Holly, then I don't see that any crime was committed."

"Perhaps not." Irma Jenner smiled sadly. "It's just that Mr. Jenner is a very proud man. A leader in this community. I doubt that he even wants to catch them but feels that he ought to make a show."

"I hope that's the case," Longarm said. "Frenchy already has me and a couple others on his backtrail. Things could get crowded."

"Please find Holly. Tell her that we would welcome her back with open arms. She belongs with her own kind. We're family."

"I'll tell her, ma'am," Longarm said, even as he thought that any woman who was bold enough to run away with Frenchy in the night would probably be the kind of woman who would not bend to the idea of marrying a man who already had a passel of wives and kids.

Longarm arose before dawn the next morning, and had no trouble following the road that led westward off the mountains and down into the Great Salt Lake Valley. He angled toward distant Salt Lake City, and hoped that he would find Frenchy and the Perry girls and that he could arrest them all without a fuss.

Arriving in Salt Lake City, Longarm went straight to the sheriff's office and asked for the lawman's help.

"Well, Marshal," Sheriff Elias Williams said, "I keep a pretty close touch on what goes on in town, and I can tell

126

you that we've not been troubled by anyone matching the descriptions that you've given me. Are you sure that they came here?"

"No," Longarm admitted, "I'm not."

"Maybe they bypassed us. Might have ridden our railroad north to Ogden and boarded the Union Pacific Railroad for places unknown farther west."

"That's quite possible."

"Then again," Williams said, "they might have ridden south. Only thing we know for sure is that they probably didn't backtrack into the Wasatch Mountains or go due west into the lake itself."

"That's a fact," Longarm said. "But I have to consider the welfare of this Mormon girl Frenchy hooked up with in Purity. Her name was Holly. She wasn't married to Mr. Jenner. In fact, he was her uncle and she was just staying with that family until she could sort her life out and decide what she was going to do after her husband died. But everyone expected her to marry into that household."

"That would have made sense," the sheriff said with complete confidence. "A widow woman needs to find a good husband. I know Robert Jenner and he's a fine, God-fearin' man. I'm sure that the widow would have been well cared for in the Jenner household."

"That may be the truth," Longarm said, "but perhaps being 'well cared for' just wasn't enough for a pretty young woman like Holly."

Sheriff Williams cleared his throat. He was as tall as Longarm, but ten years older and no doubt a church elder. "Now see here," he began, "I think the best thing that you can do is to let the membership of our church take care of our own affairs."

"Frenchy Lemond escaped from a federal courthouse in Colorado. His accomplices, the two women I mentioned, murdered a bailiff and shot me and my boss with the full intention of killing us too. This isn't a 'church affair,' Sheriff Williams. It's a matter of federal law and I mean to arrest and return those three to stand trial back in Colorado."

"Just return the girl to me," the sheriff advised. "And if you come across Mr. Jenner and his friends, I'd advise you to leave them alone and let me handle things."

Longarm had no intention of meeting this request. "There is also some confusion about missing money."

"She stole his money?"

"No. It was the girl's own money. After her husband died, it came from the sale of their properties."

"I doubt that," the sheriff said. "I'd bet that the money belonged to Mr. Jenner."

"Why?" Longarm demanded, feeling his temper rising.

"I just have a feeling that the girl was still so upset by losing her husband that she just lost her better judgment when she ran away with that scoundrel."

Longarm could see that he was not going to get any support from this man. Still, he took the trouble to write Billy Vail's name and Denver address on a sheet of paper. "If you hear of any of the three that I'm seeking, I wish you'd send a a telegram to this man right away. He'll know what to do."

The sheriff took the paper, glanced at it, and then tossed it on his desk. "Sure thing."

Longarm didn't believe him. The sheriff's obvious indifference left little doubt in Longarm's mind that Williams would pitch Billy's name and address in his trash basket the minute Longarm was out of sight.

"Tell me," the sheriff said when Longarm reached the door on his way out, "are you going north to Ogden, or south?"

"I haven't decided yet."

The sheriff smiled in a manner that was meant to be open and guileless, but was not. "Why don't you let me know when you do decide."

"Sure thing," Longarm said, mocking the other's response to the slip of paper with Billy Vail's name and office on it.

Out on the street, Longarm removed a cheroot from his coat pocket and jammed it into his mouth. He didn't bother to light the cigar, but instead chewed it a little as he strode down the avenue toward his horses. When remounted, he hesitated for a few moments, looking first north in the direction of Ogden, then south towards Provo.

Acting purely on a hunch, he reined south. It was his full intention to stop at every little town and village along the way and ask people if they'd seen Frenchy Lemond and the Mormon girl he'd taken up with. And if they hadn't seen that pair, what about the Perry girls? They were the kind that would not be overlooked and would be long remembered.

Near the outskirts of Salt Lake City, Longarm reined up and twisted around in his saddle. He could see the Mormon Temple, which was still in construction and topped by a gold-leaf-covered statue of the Angel Moroni. The city itself was a model of order and cleanliness, and the surrounding farms were a testimony to the hard work and dedication that the Mormon people had put into creating their Zion where Brigham Young had led them in 1847 after years of persecution in the East. Longarm had had his differences with the Mormons, who had never

129

bent to the yoke of federal law, but he certainly admired their hard work and clean living.

Provo was a thriving farm community on the south bank of the Provo River. The sheriff there was cooperative and Longarm finally got a break.

"Yep," the man said, "I saw them two blond women pass through. They were traveling in a buggy."

"A buggy?"

"That's right. They looked as pretty as you please too. I asked them if I could help them and they just laughed and said no, thank you."

"Did you happen to ask them where they were heading?"

"I did not. However, they did ask me about the lay of the land to the south."

"And you told them?"

"I told them that it was a bountiful land with many small Mormon communities and fine people."

"And they said?"

The sheriff shrugged. "Like you, they were interested in knowing if I'd seen this Frenchy Lemond fella. They described him. I said that I had not but that others were looking for a man a lot like him, someone who called himself Mr. French."

"That would be Mr. Jenner and the other men from Purity."

"Yes, I suppose it would." The sheriff smiled. "Marshal, it seems to me that this Frenchy fella is attracting people like a magnet. What's going to happen if you all overtake the man at once?"

"Damned if I know," Longarm said. "It depends on Frenchy. If he thinks that I will be able to protect him from the Purity menfolk and from the Perry girls, then he might surrender."

"And if he doesn't?"

"He'll fight," Longarm said with certainty. "Frenchy lives by his own code of honor and that code usually revolves around a woman."

"Like the girl he kidnapped from Purity."

"I doubt that Frenchy kidnapped her," Longarm said. "It just isn't his style."

And with that, Longarm thanked the man, gave him Billy Vail's name and address, then climbed on his horse and headed south hoping to cross Frenchy's trail before the Mormons caught and hanged the man.

Chapter 14

"Yes sir, Deputy Marshal," the traveling drummer said from atop his wagon. "I saw 'em riding west straight over them low hills."

"All of them? Are you sure?"

"Hell, yes, I'm sure. It's been a regular land stampede across this wilderness. First was the Frenchman and his woman. Next was two blond whores a-whippin' their buggy horses and going like the wind. Then yesterday about sundown, I saw this bunch of Mormons come sniffin' along them other folks' tracks like a hound dog on a coon's scent."

Longarm's eyes reached to the west. "How big a lead did the Frenchman have on the gals in the buggy?"

"About half a day."

"And Perry sisters on the posse of Mormons?"

"Another day. Maybe even a day and a half."

The drummer, a tall, gangly man in his fifties with mutton-chop whiskers and a wide, phony grin, scratched himself and added, "The two sisters asked about the Frenchman, and they sure seemed upset when I told them that he had another woman. Don't know why, though. Them yellow-haired whores sure looked good to me. I told them that, if they were looking for a good man, they needn't look any farther."

"And they said?"

The drummer grinned sheepishly. "Well, I don't think I'll tell you what they said. But let's just say it wasn't the most flattering thing a man would ever hear about hisself."

"I'll bet," Longarm said with a wry grin. "But before you go having all kinds of regrets, you ought to know that those two women are wanted for murder in Colorado."

The drummer's jaw dropped. He finally closed his mouth and gulped. "Is that a fact?"

"I'm afraid that it is. One more question. Did any of them say where they were heading?"

"Well, the Frenchman asked how far it was to Gold Peak, Nevada. Then he asked if the strike was still going strong in Candelaria."

"And you told him?"

"I told him that Candelaria was still a roaring boom town. As for Gold Peak, well, I heard the ore played out real quick and everyone moved on."

"Thanks," Longarm said, spurring his mount forward and feeling much better about things now that he knew for certain that he was on the right trail.

As he rode west into central Nevada, the land became increasingly arid and lonesome. This was still Paiute country, and although those treacherous Indians had been defeated during the Paiute Wars of the 1850's, there were still random murders throughout the territory by both whites and Indians. The Paiutes had long contended that the whites, in cutting down their pinyon trees for fuel and mine tunnel bracings, were depriving them of their food staple. Longarm knew this to be true. Pinyon nuts had always been the mainstay of their diet.

133

Overrun by miners and prospectors, the Paiutes had been forced onto reservations but, like the Apache, they had never really admitted defeat and were apt to cause trouble whenever they saw opportunity to strike back at their white oppressors.

Longarm knew that Frenchy, in his haste to leave Utah and all pursuit far behind, might very well be riding into Indian trouble. After all, what could be more tempting to a band of angry Paiute warriors than a couple of whites riding three trail-weary horses? Such easy prey could be slaughtered and their bodies hidden never to be found again.

"You'd better be careful," Longarm said aloud as his keen eyes surveyed the empty, desolate vistas. "Frenchy, your life might not be worth much if I catch you again, but that young woman's life is entirely another matter."

Seventy miles to the west, and in the shade of a cutback, Frenchy was locked in Holly's passionate embrace. Their horses were picketed nearby, and one of them watched absently as Frenchy and the young Utah widow coupled on a sweat-stained horse blanket. It wasn't a thing that either of them had planned, but neither of them had had the power to stop once their parched lips had finally met.

"I never dreamed it could feel so wonderful," Holly panted, her slender body coated with sweat. "Never!"

"Neither did I," Frenchy grunted, his hips pistoning in and out as he expertly worked over the girl. "I'm going to teach you things you'd blush even to dream about."

"I never had a man like you," Holly moaned, her head turning back and forth as she struggled to catch her breath.

She could not control her legs. Her heels were creating furrows in the sand and her bottom was shaking like crazy. She felt as if her heart would burst and while she wanted him to stop, she kept begging him for more. It was crazy and it was wonderful what he was doing to her body. She felt like the Frenchman had turned a key and opened up something inside that she had never dreamed could exist or feel so good!

"What are you doing!" she cried. "Stop! No. Don't stop. Don't *ever* stop!"

"I'm doing what ought to have been done to you a long time ago," he grunted with teeth drawn back from his lips.

Holly grabbed and hugged him as she felt her body begin to buck uncontrollably. She was like a leaf about to be torn from the safe haven of its tree. She was a ship about to be tossed by a storm onto the rocks. She was about to go insane with this feeling! She could not stop thrashing, and incoherent words poured from her lips.

"Come on, baby!" he shouted. "You've been waiting years for this!"

"Yes!"

Frenchy laughed even as he felt fire searing his testicles and his own control dissolve.

"Please stop!" Holly gasped, her eyelids fluttering as her body and her mind disengaged and became separate things. Holly shouted at the empty Nevada sky and her legs locked around the laughing Frenchman's waist as she felt him begin to flood her with torrents of his seed.

Frenchy could not stop his hips from driving into the woman, and when he was finally spent, he lowered himself to her and lay still for a long, long time. Something had been different this time—he was sure of it. Unbidden, tears of joy stung his eyes and unrehearsed words poured from his heart.

"I love you, Holly," he confessed to his own amazement. "I love you more than I've ever loved any woman before. You're more than life to me now. And no matter what happens to us, having made love to you, my darling, I'll never be the same."

Holly wept with happiness. "I love you too. I loved you from the very moment I first laid eyes on you building that fence up in Purity."

And so they held each other until the sun moved across the horizon and its fierce glare seared their naked bodies.

"My darling," Frenchy finally whispered, "we have to get dressed and somehow push on."

"Are we lost?"

"I don't think so. But it's been many years since I was through this country. I can't say for sure."

"I believe you will get us safely through this," she told him, her eyes bright with trust. "We can't possibly fail now that we have each other's love."

Frenchy raised his chin. "Yes," he said, climbing to his feet and reaching for his clothes. "Our love gives us new strength."

"We just have to find water," Holly said. "And we will!"

"We will," he repeated.

But by late afternoon they still had not found water and, if anything, the desert was drier and more desolate. Frenchy uncorked his canteen and shook it. "Not much left," he said apologetically.

Holly nodded. They had been rationing water for days while hoping to stumble across a spring or a small desert creek, but to no avail. Now, with their horses visibly suffering, they had seen the tracks of Indian ponies and knew that they faced a second and perhaps even more immediate threat.

Holly uncorked her own canteen. She turned it up and took just a sip, then dismounted and poured a precious little into her cupped hand for the horse she rode. The animal was so thirsty it actually bit at her and spilled the water.

"You're wasting it that way," Frenchy said.

"Well we've got to give them something!"

"We will. The last time I was on this road, it was heavily used by ore wagons. But now, I'm afraid that it's been abandoned. Even so, I'm sure that the mining camp of Dry Creek is still populated."

"How far is it?"

Frenchy sighed and licked his cracked lips. "I dunno," he admitted. "I thought we'd have come upon it by now. It can't be much farther to the west. The only thing that we can do is to keep pushing on."

"If we don't find water soon," Holly promised, "I don't think that these horses can keep going."

"They'll make it through the night," Frenchy said. "After that . . . well, let's just pray for the best."

But Frenchy and Holly rode through sundown and another night without finding either water or Dry Creek. By morning, their three horses were unable to continue walking.

"Get down," Frenchy said quietly as he helped his lover from her saddle.

"What . . . you're not going to shoot them!"

"Darling, I must," Frenchy replied, savagely yanking a rifle from the saddle boot. "To do anything less would be to allow them to suffer."

Holly's mouth formed a protest, but Frenchy quickly shot the first two horses, dropping them each with a single bullet. But the third animal bolted and ran off a short distance before it stopped, lowered its head, and snorted at the scent of fresh blood.

Frenchy swore to himself. He could not, in good conscience, allow the poor beast to go on suffering. Levering another shell into his rifle, he started after the horse, but stopped dead in his tracks when he saw a movement on the horizon.

"What is it!" Holly cried, shading her eyes from the bright sun.

"It's a . . . a buggy!" Frenchy cried, hope lifting his spirits to the sky, only to plummet like a rock when he said, "Oh, my God, it's Loretta and Sophie!"

"Who?"

Frenchy turned to Holly in a state of near panic because he did not know what the Perry girls would do to them. No doubt they would be filled with vengeance because he had left them in Laramie. And when they saw sweet, delicate Holly, the woman he now loved, they would be consumed with jealousy.

"Look," he said quickly. "These women are hard and dangerous. Just claim that . . . that you're my sister."

"What!" Holly cried. "I can't do that!"

"Then tell them . . . tell them whatever you want except don't tell them we are lovers. That we plan to become man and wife."

Holly stared at him in amazement. "You're afraid of these women?"

"They're vipers," he said, levering a shell into the breech of his rifle. "They may try to shoot me down on sight. You must stay away from me until I can calm them down. Just . . . just don't say anything."

"All right," Holly said, finally understanding.

When the Perry girls reined in their buggy their eyes fixed on the Frenchman, and it was Loretta who broke the icy silence. "You left Sophie and me for that skinny, flat-chested wench!"

"No," Frenchy said. "I left alone."

"Why, you smooth-talking sonofabitch!" Sophie hissed, her hand clenching a six-gun that rested in her lap.

"I was sure that we were being followed," Frenchy said. "And I thought that the only way to keep you girls from being captured was to leave you. It broke my heart, but I knew that it was something that had to be done."

"Bullshit!" Loretta said, raising a shotgun and pointing it at Frenchy. "We saved your ass and then you run out on us!"

Frenchy gulped. Sweat beaded on his forehead. He glanced at Holly and said, "This is . . . is a girl I saved from marrying a polygamist. She just wanted to get away from the man."

Sophie snorted. "You're a liar, Frenchy Lemond! You took her for the same reason you always take women."

"That's not true!" Holly cried, rushing between the buggy and Frenchy. "My husband had died and my uncle was going to force me to marry him so that he could take all my money."

"You got money?" Loretta asked.

Holly swallowed. "Yes. Some. It came from the sale of my late husband's land and livestock."

"How much!" Sophie demanded.

Frenchy took a step forward. "You're not taking her money!"

Loretta cocked back one of the hammers of her shotgun. "Another step, another word, and I'll blow a hole in you big enough to drive this buggy through, Frenchy. And you know that I'm not one to bluff."

"Yeah, I know."

"Now," Loretta said, almost sweetly. "Honey, how much is sweet-talking Frenchy worth to you? If he ain't worth much, then me and Sophie mean to castrate and leave him right here for the buzzards."

Holly paled. "I . . . I have eight hundred dollars. That's all that I have but you can have it all! Just please don't hurt Frenchy. We're in love."

Frenchy groaned and the Perry sisters cackled meanly. Finally Sophie glanced sideways at Loretta. "You think it's worth eight hundred dollars to give up the satisfaction of killing that fast-talking two-timing snake?"

"I guess it might be," Loretta said. "But barely."

"Get your money, honey!"

"Holly, no!" Frenchy protested.

But Holly did get her money, and then she rushed up to the buggy and shoved it at the two women. "Could we please have some water? I see you've got a water barrel in the buggy and—"

Loretta snatched the money from Holly's hand even as Sophie fired at Frenchy. She missed, and the Frenchman dove behind brush as Loretta's shotgun belched smoke and flame. A moment later, the buggy was racing on up the old abandoned road and they heard Sophie's laughter and mocking voice yell, "Roast in hell, the both of you!"

Frenchy jumped up and the rifle in his hands banged three times. The buggy disappeared over a low rise and Frenchy lowered his weapon with grim satisfaction. "I guess they'll play hell keeping that water barrel from leaking dry."

Holly threw her arms around Frenchy and began to cry. And standing there in that awful, desert desolation, Frenchy damn near cried too.

Chapter 15

Since Frenchy's last horse hadn't stayed around to be shot, and now seemed to want to tag along after them, they offered the suffering animal a handful of their precious remaining water.

"Holly, you ride this horse until it drops. I'll follow along on foot as best I can."

"I won't go on ahead without you," she vowed. "We're in this mess together and we're going to get out of it together or not at all."

Frenchy's heart filled with love and pride for this valiant Mormon girl. "I wish I'd a found you when I was about sixteen years old," he told her. "If that had happened, we'd most likely have a passel of kids and a nice house. Maybe a business or farm too."

"We still can have all those things," Holly told him as she mounted the faltering horse. "I'm not giving up on any of it, my wonderful Frenchy."

But her pluck could not lift his own low spirits. "I'm afraid that I've always brought bad luck to every woman I ever had anything to do with. It started with my mother, who died giving me birth."

"That wasn't your fault."

"I'm accursed when it comes to women."

"Not to me you're not!" Holly reached down and her fingers brushed his cheeks. "Frenchy, I loved my first husband. He was a good man. I'd have been happy to be married to him the rest of my days. But it wasn't meant to be. We had plans and dreams and now they're nothing. I thought that my life was over until you arrived in Purity, and then I knew that I could still dare to believe in happiness."

His throat tightened painfully. "This husband that you loved, he was a good man?"

"A wonderful man. Kind and considerate. We were only married for sixteen months. I was very happy."

There was a long pause while Frenchy considered this. Finally he blurted out what was on his mind. "But wouldn't he have taken other wives?"

"No!" Holly lowered her voice. "Not all Mormon men believe in polygamy. It's been a curse to us, and I predict the day will come when it is no longer officially sanctioned among the leaders of our people. Joseph Smith and Brigham Young are dead now, and the new church leaders are beginning to speak against the vile practice. Men like Mr. Jenner cling to the past. But they are the last of the old breed and their numbers are dying out."

"Well," Frenchy said, "I'm glad to hear that. Personally I've never been man enough to handle even one woman, let alone a bunch of wives."

"How did you ever get involved with those two . . . women?"

"It's a long, sad story," Frenchy told her. "And one I'd just as soon not go into."

"Then I'll never speak another word on it the rest of our days together," Holly promised.

Frenchy stopped and turned in a full circle, his eyes

skipping across the hot, arid wasteland. "I'd say that . . . Holy Jeezus! Look, Holly!"

Holly twisted around on the back of the horse and gasped to see the cloud of dust rooster-tailing up into the pale, cloudless sky. She started to jump down off the horse but Frenchy cried, "No! Run this horse as far as he can go and I'll try to hold off the Indians."

"Maybe they're not Indians."

"Who else could they be?"

Frenchy's question was answered only a few minutes later when Holly cried, "Lord have mercy! It's Mr. Jenner and some of the men from Purity!"

"Holly, git!"

But Holly wouldn't run. Instead, she jumped down from her suffering mount, snatched Frenchy's sixgun from his holster, and declared, "We're standing together. I'd rather die than leave you and be forced to marry Robert Jenner."

One glance at her told Frenchy that it would be futile to argue. So he planted his feet and checked his rifle. There was little doubt that he was going to be shot. The only positive thing that he could think of was that there were no trees suitably tall enough to allow a hanging.

Robert Jenner was in the lead and when he saw Holly and Frenchy, he drew his gun and urged his mount into a hard run. At a hundred yards, he fired without hope of hitting his target. An instant later, he saw Frenchy drop to one knee, punch his rifle to his shoulder, take aim, and fire. Jenner felt the slug whip-crack across the side of his face, and he yelped as most of his right ear disappeared.

"I'm hit!" he screamed, dragging his horse to a stand-still as his companions bailed off their mounts and reached for their own rifles.

143

"Don't shoot or you'll hit Holly!" Jenner shouted, holding a bleeding tag of what had been his ear. "Dammit, don't shoot or you'll kill her for certain!"

The others held their fire. One, a quiet man named Charles Holter, said, "If we aren't going to try and put a bullet through him, then what are we supposed to do?"

Jenner grimaced. He was bleeding profusely and even his thick, insensitive blacksmith's fingers could tell that there wasn't enough ear left to bother with. Just a piece that dangled by a thread of loose flesh.

"Yeah," another Mormon said. "What are we going to do now?"

"Maybe he'll surrender," Jenner said, teeth gritted in pain.

"I doubt that very much," Charles said. "After kidnapping your cousin and stealing your money? He's not stupid. You said that yourself, Robert."

"Yeah, yeah. I know. But let's try and talk to him. Maybe Holly has come to her senses by now. Maybe I'll take her, my money, and his horse and we'll leave him out here without water. It'd be a far worse fate than a hanging."

"I doubt he'll consent to that," Charles said. "He's a desperate man."

"Better we try and talk him into showing sense," Jenner said doggedly. "No reason for any of us to get killed and leave behind fatherless children and grieving widows."

The others readily agreed. They were thirsty, worried about Indians, and also nearly out of water. Never before had they ridden so long or so far on a manhunt. And though all were reluctant to admit it, all they really wanted to do was return alive to their mountain community of Purity.

"You watch yourself!" John Markle warned. "This Mr. French might have just gotten lucky with his first shot, but then again, maybe he really meant to put a bullet through your ear."

"That has already occurred to me," Jenner growled. "But if he guns me down, don't bother worrying about Holly. Just open fire and kill him!"

The four Mormons from Purity, Utah, nodded.

Jenner waved his bloodstained handkerchief at Frenchy. "Throw down your rifle and we'll talk!"

"Go to hell!" Frenchy yelled. "We're not surrendering to a thief!"

"Robert, what does he mean by that?" Charles Holter asked.

"I have no idea."

"Well, let's find out."

Frenchy could feel his heart pounding as the Mormons remounted their horses and rode forward with Jenner slightly out in front. "That's far enough," Frenchy called when they were within fifty yards.

The horsemen reined in. Jenner leaned forward in his saddle, a big man on a stout horse that showed the effects of the long manhunt. "Mr. French, you stole my wife-to-be and her money. You're going to have to—"

"That's a lie!" Holly cried. "I told you that I wouldn't marry you. I told everyone in your household that I'd known love and I would not become your wife."

"Holly, now you just—"

"Let me finish. I would never marry you, and the money you want so badly is mine! It belonged to me and my husband and you're not getting a cent of it."

Charles glanced sideways at Jenner. "Her story sure don't square with yours, Robert."

"She's lying!" Jenner choked. "That outsider, well, he's . . . he's addled her mind!"

"Addled my mind! Why you . . . you greedy, lying mon-

145

ster! I never wanted to marry you. I wouldn't be your wife if you were the last man on earth. All you wanted was my money. Even Irma told me that."

John Markle scowled. "Holly, are you . . . all right?"

"Of course I am! And I'll tell you something else." She paused, then surprised everyone by smiling at Jenner. "Robert, grab hold of your saddlehorn or you're going to take a fall."

"What are you talking about!"

"I'm talking about money. It's gone. All of it. I don't have a penny left."

Jenner blinked. "What!"

"It was stolen," Holly proclaimed almost happily. "Two women in a buckboard came by and took every cent I had. Eight hundred dollars."

Jenner paled. His eyes jumped past Holly and followed the fresh set of buggy tracks west.

"We've been following them too," Charles Holter said. "Who were they?"

Frenchy sighed and started to explain, but Holly cut him off short by saying, "I never saw them before. They just robbed us of everything."

"I don't believe you!" Jenner exclaimed, seeming to recover at last. "It's a lie!"

"It's the truth!" Holly threw her satchel at Jenner. "Search through that. You won't find any money. Search *us*! No money again. I tell you, we were robbed and I haven't a cent. You're too damned late."

Robert Jenner rifled the contents of the satchel and then he turned it upside down spilling everything into the dirt road. No money.

His mouth turned down at the corners. "I don't want you back! I offered you my home and you took my money and ran off with this . . . this outlaw."

146

And then, before anyone could say another word, the Mormon sawed on his reins and turned his horse about.

"Ya!" he shouted, booting his mount into a heavy gallop.

There was a long, awkward silence, not broken until Charles Holter said, "Holly, I guess it's your word against Robert's. I believe him, not you. But one cancels out the other."

"He's a liar," Holly said, the heat gone from her voice. "But it doesn't matter to me what any of you believe. Not anymore it doesn't."

"We'd still like to have you back," John Markle said. "We'll escort you back to Salt Lake City. You'll be taken care of. You'll never want for food or shelter."

"Only for love," Holly said, lowering her gun and slipping her arm through Frenchy's. "Go back where you came from. This is finished."

"My family will pray for you," a young man named Edward Whipple said, turning his horse around to ride after the others.

"We could use some water!" Frenchy shouted. "If you don't leave us some water, you'll be responsible for us dying!"

Whipple drew up his horse. He looked back over his shoulder and stared at them. "I'm carrying two," he said, untying one of his canteens. "This one's full. Good luck to you both."

The man dropped the canteen and rode on to catch up with his friends. Holly and Frenchy both ran over to the canteen and they each took a long, lovely drink.

"Now a little for the horse. Please?" Holly asked.

"All right," Frenchy said, watching the Mormons ride away. "Only the last time the horse bit you. I'll do it this time."

"Fine," Holly said, watching the Mormons ride back toward Utah. "Edward was always a sweet man with a big heart."

"Maybe you should have married him," Frenchy said in a flash of petty jealousy.

"I would have if he'd asked me. But he deferred to my uncle's wishes and so I was saved to love you."

Frenchy's heart melted at those words. He took Holly into his arms and kissed her, their lips as dry and scaly as the belly of a horned toad. Even so Frenchy felt a stir of passion. And if there had been any shade about, he would have spread their horse blanket on the sand and joyfully taken Holly all over again.

Chapter 16

Longarm saw the Mormon horsemen from Purity a good half hour before they were aware of his presence. Since they were coming back toward Utah, Longarm considered it a real possibility that they had already overtaken and executed Frenchy. If that were the case, Longarm knew he had a tough decision to make. The Mormons, no matter what their contentions, were not sworn officers of the law and had no powers to kill Frenchy.

Longarm touched his heels to his horse and galloped ahead to meet the men from Utah hoping that they had just given up the chase.

The Mormons reined in their sweaty horses when they saw Longarm riding one buckskin and leading a second. They were heavily armed and suspicious, especially given Longarm's disreputable image. He was dirty and unshaven and his eye patch gave him a decidedly roguish appearance.

"Who are you!" Jenner shouted, his rifle up and ready.

"Deputy Marshal Custis Long out of the Denver Office!" Longarm showed them his badge. "I'm on the trail of Frenchy Lemond and two women who gunned down a bailiff in the Denver federal courthouse." He briefly described the fugitives. "Have you seen them?"

Jenner grinned. "You say his name if Frenchy Lemond? What's he done?"

"Where is he?" Longarm asked, pointedly ignoring the man's question.

Jenner turned around in his saddle. He was smiling when he said to his companions, "I told you that man was an outlaw."

"Where is he?" Longarm repeated, his patience already wearing thin.

"You ought to overtake him by nightfall," Jenner said. "He's in bad shape. He shot two horses and the third one is dying. He's on foot."

"And you left him to die of thirst out here?" Longarm demanded.

"I gave them a full canteen," Edward Whipple said quickly.

"Them?" Longarm said.

"He's got one of our people with him," Jenner replied. "A widow, Mrs. Holly Felton."

"Maybe we'd better go back and help Deputy Long arrest that man and then bring Holly back," Whipple suggested. "It'd be the right thing to do."

"It would be the *wrong* thing to do," Longarm said. "Frenchy Lemond is a dangerous man with nothing to lose. The last thing I either want or need is for you people to be cluttering up my arrest."

"Now just a minute there!" Jenner said angrily. "Mrs. Felton is one of our people and we have a responsibility to her."

"I'll see that she has a safe return," Longarm promised, deciding there was nothing to be gained by adding that Holly was a free woman with the legal right to make

150

her own decision whether or not she wished to return to Purity.

"Are you sure that you don't want our help?"

"I'm sure," Longarm replied, pointing down at the road. "Did you see who was driving the buggy that made those tracks?"

"No, sir," Jenner said. "We'd been wondering about them ourselves."

"Thanks," Longarm said, tipping his hat and riding past the men.

"I want her back in Purity!" Jenner shouted after Longarm. "Not Salt Lake City—Purity!"

Longarm tugged his hat down and kept riding. He wasn't going to say anything, but he could not understand how those men had, in good conscience, abandoned Frenchy and the Felton woman on foot with only a single canteen of water in a wilderness still threatened by marauding bands of Indians.

It was almost sundown when he saw the overturned buggy with its dead horses. When he got a little closer, he saw Frenchy and someone else carrying rocks to pile over what were obviously graves. Longarm spurred his weary horses into a run, and when Frenchy heard the sound of hoofbeats, the man spun around, dropped a boulder, and jumped for his rifle.

Longarm brought his horses to an abrupt stop. He yanked his rifle out of its saddle scabbard and hit the ground in a running dismount. A bullet whistled past him as he dove for the cover of some nearby rocks. When he lifted his head, another slug sent his Stetson sailing.

"Damn you, Frenchy! I'm taking you back to Denver!"

"Longarm?"

"That's right!"

There was a moment of silence as Frenchy digested this news. "I'm glad that you weren't killed in that courtroom!"

"Somehow," Longarm shouted, "I find that damned hard to believe!"

"But it's the truth! We're friends! Remember, you owe me your life!"

Longarm scowled because it galled him to be in debt to anyone, much less the man that he was sworn to deliver to a hangman's noose.

"Give it up, Frenchy! I know that you're low on water and afoot! You can't win! Surrender and I'll see that no harm comes to you!"

"Ha! I'd rather die of a bullet right now than dance at the end of a rope!"

Longarm could see the logic of Frenchy's reasoning. Given Frenchy's situation, he'd have preferred to fight it out too. Especially considering that Frenchy was an excellent marksman with both pistol and rifle. Longarm figured that he had the experience and fighting edge, but not by much.

"What about the young woman?"

"What about her?"

"Why don't you let her go? I'd hate for her to catch a stray bullet!"

Longarm waited for a response that was slow in coming. He could hear Frenchy and the young woman as they argued vehemently. The sun began to slide into the western hills and the sky glittered like polished brass.

"Frenchy!" Longarm shouted. "What's it going to be?"

"You'll have to come and get us!" Frenchy answered at last.

Longarm swore in anger, though he admitted Frenchy's response should not have surprised him. It was just that he had little stomach for killing Frenchy Lemond because he did owe the man his life.

"What happened to Loretta and Sophie?"

"They're both dead!"

Longarm raised up a little. Though the fading light, he could see that Frenchy and the Mormon woman had taken cover behind the overturned buggy. "What happened?"

"I don't know! I think it was a band of roving outlaws and cutthroats! Someone chased them and their buggy overturned! Loretta was crushed under the buggy! Sophie—well, they made her die hard! We been trying to get them buried!"

Longarm slumped back down behind his cover. He needed to think about this.

"Longarm!"

"Yeah!"

"You need to remember that it wasn't me that opened up with a shotgun and dropped that poor bailiff! I never shot anyone except in a fair fight! Why don't you tell your boss that I was killed along with Loretta and Sophie? I'll even pile a third row of rocks up so it'll look like another grave! No one will know the difference!"

There was a long, tense silence. Then Longarm replied, "*I'd* know, Frenchy!"

"But you wouldn't have to tell anyone!"

Frenchy was right. Maybe what he said even made excellent sense. But Longarm couldn't quite swallow the idea. After all, he was sworn to do his duty and his duty was to bring in the fugitive Frenchman.

"Longarm, listen to me! Holly and I are going to get married if we get out of this damned desert alive! We're going to have a family!"

"He's telling the truth!" Holly cried, her voice cracked and desperate. "We love each other!"

153

"I'm happy for you," Longarm shouted, "but that hasn't got a thing to do with what I've *got* to do!"

"Dammit, Longarm!" Frenchy shouted. "We'll even agree to name our firstborn son after you! All you have to do is ride away and give us a chance to make it to civilization before whoever killed Sophie and Loretta returns!"

"Please!" Holly begged.

Longarm absently brushed a hand across his eyes. In all his years of being a deputy federal marshal, he had never been caught in such an agonizing dilemma where duty was concerned. If Frenchy was going to get married, that meant he very well might stop romancing other men's wives. No guarantees, but Longarm knew that Frenchy— despite his many faults relative to women—actually possessed a rigid gentleman's code of honor. And Longarm had a hunch he would not cheat on a wife. That meant that his womanizing days might actually come to an end. No more jealous husbands or lovers. No more killings.

"How about it?" Frenchy shouted.

Longarm cussed himself. "Sorry, Frenchy! I've got to take you in!"

There was a long silence before Frenchy said with great resignation, "Then you're going to have to kill me before I kill you!"

So, Longarm thought. This was how it would end. The Perry girls were dead, and now either he or Frenchy would also die before this night was over. Neither of them would wait until morning. Somewhere out on this starlit expanse of desert sage, creosote brush, and rocks, one of them would kill the other and the issue would resolve itself.

Longarm waited until the darkness deepened. Then he inched back to his buckskins and used his Stetson as a vessel to hold water for them both that he poured from his canteen. Taking a long drink for himself, he studied the dark silhouette of the land, and decided that the shallow dry wash to his right would be as good a path as any to get to Frenchy.

Longarm placed his hat on his saddlehorn. If he was the one to die tonight, Frenchy and his woman would have two good horses to carry them westward. And maybe that was how this was all supposed to come out anyway. Longarm had survived a lot of gunfights and always managed to come out on top, but tonight might be another story.

Gripped by sadness and regret, Longarm had to force himself to push everything from his mind except that he was a lawman and Frenchy was a condemned killer. Never mind that he was also a friend and a decent man who had made a few grievous mistakes. Never mind that he had saved Longarm's life at the risk of his own. Never mind any of those things. It was, Longarm knew, a matter of kill or be killed.

"Let's get it done," he said to himself, knowing that, even now, Frenchy and the Mormon woman might be moving to gain the advantage.

Chapter 17

He was almost close enough to take a bite of one of the dead horses, and all at once Longarm knew that Holly Felton and Frenchy were gone. Somehow they'd managed to sneak away in the night, and now it was a matter of trying to figure out where they were hiding in ambush.

Longarm holstered his weapon, picked himself off the ground, and rushed over to the buggy. There wasn't anything to see. Just some scattered supplies and the dead horses. He would have liked to have had a good look about to see if he could read tracks and discover who had killed the Perry girls, but that would have to wait. Right now, he had to get Frenchy.

Had the man and the woman just run off? That wouldn't make much sense. After all, they'd had only one horse and, from its appearance, it had not seemed likely that the animal had enough strength or speed left to carry the pair far before collapsing.

Then where was Frenchy?

Longarm was considering that very question when he heard his buckskins start in alarm. Longarm jumped up and sprinted back toward where he'd left the animals. If

Frenchy and the woman managed to steal his horses, the game was up.

Damn! He'd left both buckskins hidden behind a low rise of land where they were certain to be out of any danger of being hit by an errant bullet. Now, as he plunged over the rise, a gun opened fire to his right. That single shot sent Longarm diving forward even as the muzzle fire from another gun blossomed on his left.

A cross fire! He'd run straight into a cross fire!

Longarm dragged his gun out and did his damnedest to burrow into the ground below the level of the stunted sage. Even so, another bullet clipped the earth only inches from his face. Longarm fired two more quick rounds to his right, then heard the sound of retreating hoofbeats. He raised his head to recognize the silhouetted outline of the Mormon woman on one of his horses while leading the second at a gallop. And there was little doubt that she was going to Frenchy and that the two would then escape into the night.

Longarm shouted, "Damn you, Frenchy!"

There was no answering challenge. The only sound Longarm heard was that of his horses' hoofbeats. Longarm cussed a blue streak. Furious at not anticipating that Frenchy would somehow convince a docile Mormon widow to use a gun, he realized he had blundered into a trap. Now there could only be one more move in this game, and that was for the woman to circle around and rescue Frenchy. And this, Longarm vowed, must not happen.

He threw caution to the wind and wheeled to his right, where he knew Frenchy had been only moments earlier. It was a desperate move because, if Frenchy was waiting, he would have a silhouetted target that he was easily capable of hitting.

So intent was Longarm on stopping the pair from reuniting and stealing his horses that he did not even hear the quick, dry whisper of rattles. He stepped on a rattlesnake and felt its hard, muscular body roll underfoot. Longarm tried to jump, but his ankle twisted and he crashed into the sage, striking his head against a rock and momentarily losing consciousness. The awful pain of the rattlesnake's fangs jabbing deeply into his thigh brought a shout that began in his throat. Longarm twisted his gun around and emptied it at the serpent, but the poisonous creature slithered into the brush. He cut a two-inch-long slit in his pants and squeezed out as much of the poison as he could, then pressed his bandana to the fang marks.

Longarm was in a bad fix. Fighting down panic, he knew that he had to reload. If he didn't reload, Frenchy would find and kill him. Longarm gritted his teeth. He had always had a fear and loathing of snakes in general and rattlers in particular. He'd seen an Indian child die from a rattlesnake bite and it had not been pretty.

Longarm rolled over onto his back and dragged his six-gun up before his one eye. He tried to focus and when that was impossible, he tore off his eye patch and gazed up at the starry heavens. Was he imagining things, or could he already feel the poison attacking his brain, making his fingers tremble?

Fighting down his rising panic, Longarm reached for his cartridge belt. Yes, the poison was affecting him. He already felt dizzy and sick. Frenchy didn't *have* to shoot him. The man and his woman had won the fight. Now all they needed to do was ride away and leave him to die or be found by the same renegades that had killed the Perry sisters.

"Sonofabitch," Longarm whispered as he fumbled for

and dropped a fresh cartridge. He tried to pry another loose from his cartridge belt, but he was partially lying on the damn thing and his vision was playing tricks on him just when he needed it the most. Overhead, the moon and stars began a lazy circle around the dark heavens, and Longarm did not know if his vision was failing because he'd removed the eye patch or because he'd been bitten. All he knew for sure was that his time had finally come and now he was facing death.

His six-gun's weight increased with each passing second, and at last it became insupportable. Longarm allowed the gun to sag to his chest. He felt slightly nauseous and very light-headed. He closed his good eye and the heavens kept spinning. He closed the eye he'd kept under a patch and saw no difference.

Longarm could feel a tingling in his leg where he'd been bitten. The tingling sensation was moving up through his body. He could feel his heart beating abnormally fast and he was breaking out in a cold sweat.

"Longarm!"

He started. Raised his gun.

"Longarm! Can you hear me?"

Longarm kept his silence. Frenchy was determined to finish him off.

"Dammit, Longarm! If you're just wounded, I won't leave you alone to die!"

Sure, Longarm thought, cocking back the hammer of his six-gun. And when the dark silhouette of Frenchy suddenly loomed up in the night, Longarm pulled the trigger of his gun.

The hammer fell on an empty chamber. Longarm tried to move, but something struck him alongside the jaw and the night shut down on him like the heavy lid of a cast-iron oven pan.

• • •

It was full daylight when Longarm awoke in the lee of the overturned buckboard. He could smell horse meat burning and when he tried to sit up, he felt sick to his stomach. Sick enough to retch.

"Easy," the attractive Mormon widow said, rushing over to his side. "Frenchy! Frenchy, he's finally awake!"

The Frenchman appeared at Longarm's side and he was smiling as if everything was perfect. "My friend, it would be a disgrace to allow a mere snake to end the life of such a famous lawman—even if you are determined to see me die."

"If you were smart, you'd be miles away by now," Longarm said, flexing his fingers and discovering the numbness was gone.

"We couldn't do that," the woman said.

"She's right. Besides, Longarm, we're going to need your help."

"A lot of good I can do anyone right now."

Frenchy's smile died. "Listen," he said, putting a hand on Longarm's shoulder. "You're a federal marshal, right?"

"Of course."

"Well, isn't it your duty to bring in whoever killed federal fugitives?"

Longarm felt as if his skull were packed with dry adobe instead of brains. He couldn't think, much less follow what Frenchy was driving at. "Spit it out."

"All right. If we help you catch whoever killed Loretta and Sophie, will you let us go in peace?"

Longarm closed his eyes. "I don't have that authority."

"Damn your authority!" Frenchy stormed. "You'll die if we leave you. I'm asking for my freedom in exchange for your life."

160

Longarm knew in his bones that he would die if he refused. Furthermore, he had no intention of dying for nothing or throwing his life away on foolish principles. He *would* die alone snakebit and without a horse or water. And even though it would be breaking his word to Billy Vail and violating his sworn duty, there was no way that he could fairly deny this request.

"All right," he finally whispered. "But only if we catch those murderers. And another thing."

"Yes?"

"I expect you to marry this woman and quit fooling around and getting into one bad fix after another."

"Agreed," Frenchy said without hesitation.

The woman grabbed Frenchy and began to sob with joy.

Longarm shook his head. "Frenchy, I swear I can't figure out how you do it."

"Maybe someday I'll teach you, eh?" the man said with a chuckle.

"I hope I live to learn your secrets," Longarm said, feeling a chill pass through his lanky frame.

Holly touched his brow. "I've doctored a snakebite before. You're strong and in good health, Marshal, and there is no doubt that you'll survive. It'll take about three days before you feel capable of travel."

"We can't wait that long," Frenchy said. "We'd die of thirst by then and so would our horses."

"But—"

"Frenchy is right," Longarm said. "We've got to find water and help."

"We will," Frenchy vowed.

Longarm looked up at the Frenchman. He had an admission to make and wanted to get it over with. "I'm glad that you didn't hang back in Denver. And thanks for not killing me last night."

Frenchy squeezed his shoulder. "I saved your life twice, but now you give me and Holly a second chance to share a good life. So we're even."

"Yeah," Longarm echoed faintly. "We're even."

After Holly cut his pants leg open a little more, she made a quick but deep cross-hatch incision in Longarm's thigh and tried to suck out more of the rattlesnake's venom. The pain was so intense that Longarm lost consciousness. He was tied in his saddle and Frenchy led his horse while the woman rode behind. Late in the afternoon, a loud retort of Frenchy's gun roused Longarm, and when he twisted around he saw the man had given his last horse a merciful death.

A short time later, they found the ruins of Dry Creek. There wasn't much left. All the buildings had been moved and so had most of the machinery. What remained was rusting tin cans, a few broken pieces of hoisting equipment, and three boarded-up mine shafts near whose entrances rested huge mountains of mine tailings.

"I remember that there was a spring about two miles to the east," Frenchy said. "That's where we can make camp."

"Then let's go," Longarm gritted. "My head feels dizzy and my ears are ringing like church bells. I don't know if it's because I'm so thirsty or because of the snake's poison."

"I feel dizzy too," Holly said. "It must be the lack of water."

So they rode through the rusting rubble and the mine fields of broken dreams until they came to a low rise. "Hold up here," Frenchy said, "while I hike up and have a look. There's a chance that the bastards that killed Loretta and Sophie are camped on the other side."

"What would we do if they were?" Holly asked fearfully. "We can't—"

"I don't know," Frenchy interrupted. "But we'd figure out something."

Longarm took a deep breath. "I'll come along."

"No," Frenchy said, taking his rifle. "You're not in any shape to help me and you might even get me in trouble."

Longarm's pride was stung, but he had to admit Frenchy was right. And so he watched as the man hiked up to the rise and then flattened on the ground. Frenchy lay still for almost five minutes, and when he eased back down the slope and returned, his face was grim.

"I'm afraid that there are some Paiutes camped by the spring."

"How many?" Longarm asked.

"At least a dozen. Looks like a hunting party."

"No women or children?"

"Nope."

Longarm considered the situation. Finally he said, "Most of these desert Indians are peaceful. I don't think we can afford to wait until they move on to another camp. We *must* have water now."

"Holly, do you agree?"

"Yes. We can't afford to wait. These horses are about to drop."

"Then let's go pay these Indians a visit," Frenchy said. "We're all armed but so are they."

"They'll want a gift," Longarm said.

"They can butcher the dead horse I shot," Frenchy replied, "but we aren't about to give them your buckskins."

Longarm was glad to hear Frenchy say that because, next to food and water, they needed these horses.

163

Chapter 18

It was sundown when they topped the treeless rise and pulled their horses to a standstill above the Paiute camp. Camp dogs began to bark and when the Indians saw the three whites, they jumped for their weapons.

"Raise your hands, palms facing them in a show of peace," Longarm ordered, lifting his own hand and forcing himself to smile.

"Will they speak English?" Holly asked.

"Probably." Longarm looked to Frenchy. "Do you want to do the talking, or shall I?"

"I think I'd better," Frenchy said. "You don't look too good."

"Tell them we are hunting white outlaws," Longarm said. "Tell them we will pay for information."

"You're carrying money?"

"Yes."

"We'd better not let them think you have a lot of money," Frenchy said, "or they might just decide to take it by force."

Longarm nodded with agreement. He looked to Holly. "I know that you can use a gun, because you caught me in a cross fire."

"I shot up in air so there was no chance of killing you. I had to divert your attention from Frenchy," Holly explained. "I honestly could not take another human being's life unless it was in self-defense."

"Nice to know that now," Longarm said cryptically. "Let's go have a powwow."

Frenchy took Holly's place on the second buckskin and she rode double behind him, a sixgun clenched in her fist hidden from view.

"Just don't shoot me in the back by accident," Frenchy pleaded.

The Indians were heavily armed with old percussion Navy and Army Colts. A few had modern rifles using metallic cartridges, but their weapons looked to be in very bad shape. These Paiutes resembled the feared Apache in Arizona and New Mexico. They looked small and beaten until they started to fight, and then you found out they were brave, tough, and cunning.

"Hello!" Frenchy called. "Friends!"

The Indians had formed a battle line and at its center, holding one of the better rifles, stood a man probably in his forties, short but stocky and possessing the bearing of a leader. The Indian leader stepped forward and slowly raised his own hand in greeting. "Friends," he said, dark eyes moving back and forth over his three visitors.

"We need water," Frenchy said, speaking slowly.

"Paiute water," the leader said, no doubt seeing the ravages of thirst in the shrunken eye sockets of the buckskin horses.

"We will pay you for your water," Longarm said.

The Paiute's eyes shifted to Longarm. He saw the bloody bandage where Holly had sliced a cross-hatch mark in an attempt to suck out the snake poison. He jabbed his rifle at the bandage and his question was clear.

"Snake bite," Longarm explained.

The Indian leader strode over to Longarm and, with his free hand, yanked out his knife. Longarm didn't flinch but he heard Holly gasp.

"Easy," he warned the girl.

The Indian cut the bandage away and studied the wound. It was purplish and swollen with jaundiced lines of discoloration radiating up and down Longarm's muscular thigh. The Indian's mouth twisted down at the corners and he looked up at Longarm as if to measure his strength.

"Indian medicine fix for money."

"Good," Longarm said. "Now how about some water for ourselves and these horses?"

"Water for money. Much money."

"Now wait a minute," Frenchy began. "We—"

"How much money, Chief?" Longarm asked, cutting off Frenchy's protest.

"Ten dollars."

Longarm would have paid far more. But he was horse trader enough to know that, if he agreed too quickly, the chief would lose face among his people.

"Five dollars," he said, wishing he didn't have to waste time playing games.

"Ten dollars."

"That's too much!"

"You sick man. Paiute medicine fix leg good. Horses drink big and live. Ten dollars *good* price."

Longarm's face assumed a pained expression. He sighed, looked to his friends, and then finally said with an edge of anger in his voice, "All right, dammit! You win. Ten dollars."

The chief could not suppress a triumphant grin. "Ten more for you to drink too."

"Now wait a damned minute!" Longarm cried.

166

"Ten dollars. Everyone drink good water. Rest here with Paiute. Fill canteens! Easy worth ten dollars."

Frenchy took up the game. "Longarm, they got us over a barrel. We've no choice."

"He's right," Holly said, joining in with just the trace of a smile. "We'd better pay them the twenty dollars."

"Damn!" Longarm said with mock anger as he dragged the money out of his pants pocket and shoved it at the chief. "Here!"

The Indian beamed. He turned to his warriors and waved the money. They beamed, and whatever tension was in the air vanished like fog under hot sunlight.

It turned out the chief's name was Sito-itoc, which as near as Longarm could figure meant One Who Walks Far among the Paiutes. Fortunately the man went by the name Itoc.

Itoc was almost trampled when he tried to lead the thirst-crazed buckskins to the moss-rimmed desert spring. With a shout of anger, he jumped out of their path and the two buckskins charged the small, mossy-covered pond. Longarm, Holly, and Frenchy were not far behind. The water tasted brackish and it was not cool or clear, but Longarm knew that it was safe to drink because there was no sign of death around the isolated spring and the Indians were using the place as a camp for their hunting parties.

All that evening, while the Paiutes butchered and burned horse meat, steaming compresses were applied to Longarm's snake bite. The compresses were scalding and Longarm's leg turned scarlet. He protested vigorously, but Itoc insisted that the heat was necessary to draw out the poison that Holly had not been able to remove.

In the morning, Longarm awoke before dawn and when he gazed up at the last of the fading stars, he felt clear-headed and his vision in both eyes was perfect again. The horse meat had also given him new strength and he felt better than he had in days.

Itoc and his Paiutes proved to be good companions, and the three whites remained with the hunters for another full day. Longarm resisted any more steaming poultices, and after another full day of rest, he was ready to ride.

"These outlaws we seek," he told Itoc and his warriors. "They were six in number. Maybe seven but no more."

"You see these bad men?"

"No," Longarm admitted. "Only their tracks. They killed two white women in a buggy about twenty miles to the east."

Itoc relayed this information to his warriors, some of whom did not speak or understand the white man's language. One of the warriors, a boy of about fifteen, spoke with emotion, and it seemed clear that he had some important information to offer.

"What did he say?" Longarm asked when the boy had finished his talk.

"He say that he has seen these men. They are halfbreeds and they killed other whites."

Longarm wanted to be sure he understood correctly. "Are they halfbreeds, or Mexicans?"

There was more conversation. Finally Itoc said, "The boy says halfbreeds, but I think there are whites and maybe a Mexican. They live in a white man's settlement."

"Where?"

"That way," Itoc said, pointing north.

"Are they miners or . . . what do they do?"

Itoc asked this question, but the boy didn't know. He shrugged his thin shoulders and grinned.

"How far north? Ask him if he has seen this town," Frenchy said.

The boy *had* seen the town. It was perhaps two days' ride north.

When Longarm had heard all this, he felt better. "Chief Itoc, if you and your men will take us to this place and help us fight these bad men, I will pay you much money."

Itoc's answer was emphatic. "No!"

"But why?"

"Bad for Indian to kill white men. Too many white men. Indians die again. No good!"

"That's true," Longarm said, letting the Indians know that he understood the reasons for their steadfast refusal. Let a white man kill an Indian and it was a cause for celebration. Let an Indian kill a white man and the whole territory would be up in arms and sure that it was about to see a full-scale Indian uprising.

"We will start north tomorrow morning," Longarm said.

"Cost you . . . one hundred dollars."

Longarm sighed and began to wrangle. But his heart really wasn't in the charade. He was plenty willing to pay these poor warriors an even hundred dollars if they'd lead him to this crowd of murdering outlaws. And while his boss, Billy Vail, might think that he had gotten skinned by the Paiutes, Longarm thought it was money well spent.

Later that night, when Frenchy and the Mormon widow were about to walk out of the camp with their blankets, Longarm said, "Once this is over, you're finding a preacher. Don't forget."

"I won't forget," Frenchy vowed, pulling Holly close to his side. "And then we are going to wish you a fond farewell hoping never to see you again."

Longarm allowed himself to chuckle as he turned in to his own bedroll because the feeling was entirely mutual.

Chapter 19

The Paiutes had no horses but, like the Apache, they could rapidly travel amazing distances on foot. And now, as Longarm, Frenchy, and Holly Felton followed Itoc and his band of warriors northward, it was all that the buckskins could do to keep pace with the seemingly tireless Paiute warriors.

Longarm had chased Apache and marveled at their endurance, but only their best would have rivaled these tough Nevada Indians. The Paiutes traveled in single file, with the boy who led them at the head of the line, followed by Itoc and then the other warriors. It was all that Longarm and his companions could do to match their pace and keep from being left behind.

The day was warm and the Paiutes stopped at a second desert spring just before nightfall. When the sun set in the west, the Paiutes spread their skin robes, and some fell asleep without even bothering to eat the jerked horse meat they now carried.

"How much farther?" Longarm asked the Paiute chief.

After Itoc relayed this question, the boy pointed and said something, which Itoc related as another half day's walk.

Frenchy glanced nervously at Holly, then shifted his gaze to Longarm. "What are we going to do when we overtake them?"

"I'll try to arrest them for the murder of the Perry sisters," Longarm answered.

"Don't seem likely that they'd surrender if they outnumber us two or three to one."

"Nope."

Holly looked from one man to the other. "Wouldn't it be better to go find some sheriff and ask for his help?"

"Nope," Longarm repeated. "In the first place, this is a federal case and that means that a local sheriff won't have anything to gain by risking his neck. You see, Holly, they're paid by the people they are sworn to protect."

"What would these men be doing out in this wild country?"

Longarm had already given that some thought. "Sometimes you get a group that are so damned mean and murderous that they must live only amongst themselves. My guess is that this is a bunch of outlaws that prey on several mining towns in this part of Nevada. They probably range far and wide robbing banks and stagecoaches, then disappearing into this hard country where water is scarce and there are Paiutes who still make war."

"I see."

Frenchy frowned. "When I was hiding in Mexico, there were banditos who lived much the same way. They were pariahs, hated by all honest citizens and unwelcome wherever they might go. Those men were cruel and they would kill anyone for almost any reason. And since there was no law that would oppose them, they had a free rein to pillage and plunder at will."

Holly drew her knees up to her chin and stared into their little campfire. "You're making me very worried," she admitted. "If there are a half dozen or more of these people, how on earth can we oppose them?"

"That's a good question," Longarm said. "I'm not prepared to give you an answer. I can only say that we *must* get the drop on them. That way we can whittle down the odds in a hell of a hurry. Frenchy is very good with a gun."

"But not as good as you," Frenchy was quick to add.

"Close," Longarm replied. "Either way, we ought to be able to drop four of them before the others can clear leather."

Holly reached out and touched Frenchy's cheek. "If I should lose you . . ."

"Don't think of such things, my darling," he said. "I haven't waited so long to find the right girl only to get shot by a pack of murdering halfbreeds."

Holly smiled so radiantly that Longarm could not help but feel a tinge of envy. He'd had his share of good women, but this one was obviously special. He would have liked to know more about her. Where she had been born and if she had always been a Mormon. But such questions were too personal and so he kept them to himself. One thing was certain. Holly had chosen a new path in life and there was no going back now. Longarm just hoped that Frenchy would treat her right.

Longarm was up and about the next morning long before sunrise. He walked over to their little spring and drank deeply. This one had sweet cool water that fed down into a small meadow whose lush grass the buckskins were devouring like locusts. After greeting the two horses, Longarm hiked up on a knoll and found a seat on a rock. He rummaged around in his shirt and coat pockets until he found the stub of a cheroot and turned aside, cupping a match as he lit a smoke. Then, he settled back to watch the sun rise.

The darkness first gave way to a faint line of grayness creeping across the eastern horizon. The grayness thickened and began to chase the darkness higher and higher, until the glowing lip of the rising sun touched and gilded the eastern desert peaks. The earth blazed in a moment of spectacular glory.

A smile played unconsciously across Longarm's rugged features as he admired the beauty. He puffed contentedly as the sun spilled over the dark and distant line of mountains, pouring sunlight across the wilderness landscape. There were only a few wispy clouds in the sky and they turned honey-gold. Minutes later, the sun was full off the earth and the rugged land began to take clear shape.

So, Longarm thought, this would be a bloody day. Men would die, some with dignity, others perhaps slowly and very badly. Longarm checked and reholstered his sixgun. He still had not completely reconciled himself to allowing Frenchy Lemond go free. He was sure that Billy Vail would not approve. And there was always the chance that Frenchy might leave Holly and take up his old life. And if he killed other jealous men, their blood would be on Longarm's head.

"Nothing is certain in life," Longarm growled around the stub of his cheroot. "The only thing certain about any of this is that Frenchy would hang if I took him back to Denver."

"Marshal, you damn sure got that right!"

Longarm swung around on his rock to see Frenchy standing right behind him. He was irritated and embarrassed about having Frenchy sneak up and overhear him talking to himself like a confused old man.

"Dammit, Frenchy, you move quiet. But that's a good way to get yourself drilled."

"I know," Frenchy said with a grin. "When a man sneaks around visiting women in the night, he learns to walk soft and shoot quick."

"That had better be behind you now."

"It is," Frenchy promised. "Holly is my future."

"I'm glad that you can see that," Longarm said. "What are you going to tell Billy Vail?"

Longarm had been skirting that question ever since he'd agreed to Frenchy's terms. "I believe I'll tell Billy the truth. That we made a deal—my life for yours."

"And if he fires you and sends another marshal after me?"

"He could do that," Longarm conceded. "But I doubt he will."

"But he might."

"That's true."

"I'm going to change my name," Frenchy announced. "I've talked this over with Holly and she agrees."

"Don't tell me your new name. That way I can't be expected to tell it to Billy."

"All right." Frenchy squinted into the bright morning sky. "Longarm?"

"Yeah?"

"If I go down today in this fight, I want you to accompany Holly back to Denver and help her make a fresh start. You know, help her find a good job and make some decent friends. The kind of people you'd want a kid sister to fool around with."

"Why Denver?"

"She doesn't have a friend in the world outside of the Mormons. And if she goes back to Utah . . . well, she'll never leave. She's cut the ties that bind, my friend. She's going to need someone to help her make the change."

"I'll help her," Longarm said. "She's a fine girl. Too good for the company of either one of us rough-and-tumble sonsabitches, if you ask me."

Frenchy chuckled. "I didn't ask you, but now that you mention it, I agree. I hope that you find a girl like Holly someday. Maybe you should go live in a town like Purity."

It was Longarm's turn to grin. "I'd be about as welcome as a skunk under a church floor. No, thanks."

"Well," Frenchy said, turning away, "I just wanted to know that you'd look out for Holly if I step in front of a bullet."

"I'll look out for her."

"Anything you want if I make it and you don't?"

"Bury me deep so that varmints can't dig me up," Longarm said after a few minutes. "That, and let Billy know."

"I'll do it."

Longarm surged to his feet. The sun was up and so were the Paiutes. It was time to saddle the buckskins and ride. All this talk of doing one thing or another for a dead man was spooky.

"Let's get it done," he growled, passing Frenchy and heading back to break camp.

Chapter 20

"There it is," Longarm said, hugging the earth and gazing across the half mile of rugged country. "You can see that it's just another abandoned mining town. Nothing left but mine tailings and a few old ramshackle buildings."

"I don't seen any sign of life," Holly said, squinting against the glare of the afternoon sun.

"The outlaws might be gone. If they're not, my guess is that their horses are probably down in that riverbed marked by the line of cottonwood trees. The trees indicate some water."

"I agree," Frenchy said. "But where would the outlaws be?"

"Either with their horses, or maybe they're living inside a mine. Some of those diggings have some pretty fair-sized underground caverns. You can tell which by the size of their tailings."

"You're the one with all the experience in this sort of thing," Frenchy said. "What do we do?"

Longarm considered the question carefully. For one thing, even though the horse tracks around the capsized buggy indicated that six or seven outlaws had been in the group that had chased down and killed the Perry sisters, that did not necessarily mean that there wasn't a whole lot more in the camp just ahead. If that were the case, Longarm knew he had a very big problem.

"We'll wait until dark and sneak in on foot," he told Frenchy. "Holly, you'll stay here with the horses."

"I will not!"

"Yes, you will," Frenchy said. "If we get in trouble too big to handle, we'll need you to come running with the horses."

Holly's expression made it clear she was not happy with this arrangement, but she seemed to understand that it made the most sense. "What about the Indians?"

"I'm going to pay them off and send them on their way," Longarm said. "I was talking to Itoc earlier and he told me that his own tribe has dwindled down to no more than fifty people. Ten years ago, there were almost a thousand. That's what the discovery of the Comstock Lode has done to the Paiute."

Longarm retreated back to the dry wash where the Indians were waiting. He counted out a hundred dollars to the chief and gave it to him. "You've served us well, my friend. And now, before the killing starts, you need to go."

Curiously, Itoc seemed reluctant to leave. "Maybe we could help for more money?"

Longarm chuckled at that. "I'm not the federal treasury, Itoc. That means that I don't have a hell of a lot more money left."

"We do good job in bad fight. Maybe help you live, Longarm."

"Maybe."

Longarm realized he was facing a dilemma. He desperately needed and wanted the Indian warriors to join in this fight. Without them . . . well, the odds were not good. And yet he was acutely aware of the hysteria and the resulting backlash that would occur once it was widely known that Indians had killed white men—even if it involved friendly Paiute Indians killing outlaws. Longarm could not, in good conscience, put the lives of Itoc and his already decimated people at even greater risk.

"Tell you what," Longarm said. "You people stay here. If things go bad for us, we'll come running for your help."

Itoc nodded eagerly. "Cost you one hundred dollars."

"That'd be about my limit," Longarm said, in no mood to argue or haggle over the price even though it was expected.

"We fight good!"

"A hundred dollars would be all right, Itoc."

"Not too much for good Paiute fighters, Longarm."

"I said okay! I'll pay you another hundred dollars if we need you to bail us out of a fix. *Comprende?* Understand?"

Itoc blinked. He looked a little confused and then disappointed. The haggling had been too easy.

What was not easy was waiting for darkness. During the rest of the daylight hours, Longarm spent most of the time watching to see if there was any sign of life in the ghost town up ahead. He saw nothing, but that did not mean that the town was empty. His lawman's instincts told him quite the opposite was true.

"Frenchy, we'll stay together," he said after sunset had faded. "Holly, the horses are saddled. You know what to do if we come running with a band of them cutthroats hot on our heels."

"I know." Holly threw her arms around Frenchy's neck. "If you were to die . . . I would die as well."

Longarm couldn't believe this pair. "Let's go, Romeo," he said as he started off into the night to the sound of smacking lips.

Frenchy caught up to him, and as they marched across the sage-covered landscape the Frenchman said, "Do I detect a little jealousy?"

"Go to hell!"

"You *are* jealous."

"Shut up. Sounds carry in the desert at night."

Frenchy chuckled softly. "I can see that if I am killed tonight, you're going to take real *good* care of Holly."

Longarm growled, and the Frenchman lapsed into a grinning silence.

They circled around to the line of darkly silhouetted cottonwoods and moved down the damp, sandy riverbed. The sound of horses brought them up short.

Longarm crouched behind a fallen tree and studied the scene ahead. He saw horses, all right. They were contained in a huge rope corral among the trees. The outlaws had dug out a water hole which the subterranean river kept filled. He could not see any guards, but there was no reason that they should have been posted given the isolation of this hideout.

"First we steal their horses," Longarm decided out loud.

"Why!"

"A gift for our Indian friends," Longarm said with a tight smile. "And after we do that, even if we are killed, at least these bastards won't have the horses to keep raiding."

"How comforting," Frenchy snapped.

Longarm came to a crouch and moved swiftly to the rope corral. The horses snorted suspiciously at him, but when he untied the ropes and let them go, they seemed plenty eager to be driven down the dry, sandy riverbed. Longarm and Frenchy drove them for nearly a mile, where they were intercepted by the Paiutes.

"Take them," Longarm said to the Indian chief. "Ride 'em or eat 'em, your choice."

Itoc and his warriors were ecstatic. "This good gift, Longarm!"

"Yeah. Well, just remember that if we come running for your help."

Itoc understood. His warriors quietly gathered the dozen or so horses and led them away. Longarm was sure that there would be great feasting in the weeks ahead.

"All right," he said. "Let's find and arrest us some murdering outlaws."

"I can't arrest them!" Frenchy protested. "I'm the fella that always *gets* arrested. You know that."

"Fine, then just back me," Longarm drawled.

When they came to the first mine, it was clear that the shaft was unoccupied. But at the second mine, they could hear men talking and laughing inside.

"I wish we had those shotguns that Loretta and Sophie used in court to set you free," Longarm said, drawing his sixgun. "Them babies would make a big difference."

"So what do we do now?"

Longarm's brow furrowed in thought. "Let's wait until they go to sleep," he decided. "Groggy men suddenly roused out of a deep sleep are a lot less dangerous."

"Sounds good to me."

So they waited behind a rusty old ore cart resting next to a huge pile of tailings. Several of the outlaws came out to urinate and gaze up at the stars before they went back inside. Longarm judged that it was nearly midnight when he heard no more talk or laughter inside the tunnel.

"How are we going to keep from shooting each other in there?" Frenchy asked.

Longarm crept up to the entrance of the tunnel. He could see that the outlaws had left kerosene lanterns hanging from the roughly hewn log supports. "There's enough light to get the job done," he said.

Like snakes, Longarm had always tried to avoid tunnels and mine shafts. He felt claustrophobic inside the cold rock walls, but he pushed that uneasy feeling aside as he drew his gun and led the way up the tunnel.

He did not have far to go. The tunnel doglegged and suddenly opened into the working face of the mine, which was at the far end of a barn-sized cavern. And on the floor of the dimly lit cavern were no less than twenty sleeping outlaws, maybe a whole lot more.

"Let's get out of here!" Frenchy whispered. "We can't arrest this many."

"Got to," Longarm breathed. He looked around and his eyes came to rest on a pair of sawed-off shotguns. They looked to be the same ones that had belonged to Loretta and Sophie Perry. No doubt, after killing those women, the outlaws had taken the deadly weapons for themselves. Motioning to Frenchy, he let the man know his intentions were to gain possession of the shotguns.

Frenchy rolled his eyes but he did not lose his nerve, and tiptoed right behind Longarm across the cavern. And just when they were about to grab up the shotguns, one of the outlaws rolled in his sleep and bumped into the rock wall. Awakening with a start, he looked around and his eyes came to rest on Longarm and Frenchy.

Longarm snatched up the shotgun and jumped forward. The shotgun arched overhead in a desperate attempt to still what Longarm knew would be a warning shout.

"Hey, you—"

Longarm swatted the man across the bridge of his nose. It exploded with blood, but instead of losing his consciousness, the man howled and jumped to his feet.

Longarm belted him again, but by this time all hell was breaking loose. He heard Frenchy shout a warning and saw him dart back into the tunnel.

A bullet whizzed by Longarm's cheek and he spun around and pulled both triggers of the shotgun. Being confined in the cavern, the shotgun's explosion was deafening. Men screamed and dropped, some torn almost in half by the double load of shot. Longarm dropped the shotgun and sprinted toward the tunnel. Frenchy waited until he swept past and then he too unleashed a double load of buckshot back into the cavern.

"Let's get out of here!" Frenchy shouted.

Longarm did not need any encouragement. Even if they had killed ten men, that still left at least ten alive and that meant impossible odds. They shot out of the mine and scrambled around the mine tailings running for their lives. At the edge of the settlement, Longarm stopped and opened fire on their pursuers. He had the satisfaction of seeing a man drop before he turned and raced after Frenchy.

From out of the night galloped Holly and the Paiutes. Longarm had expected Holly and their horses, but not the Indian charge. The Paiutes, led by a howling Itoc, swept by him and struck the outlaws like a battering ram.

"Holy Jeezus!" Frenchy shouted, swinging up behind Holly.

Longarm took the reins to his buckskin and swung into the saddle. He reined back toward the town hearing screams and scattered gunfire. By the time that he reached the mine tunnel, the fight was over and there wasn't an outlaw left standing.

They dragged the bodies of the pack of Nevada cutthroats into the mine shaft and collapsed the entrance from above, sealing the shaft forever. Itoc and his warriors took their horses and all but twenty-three dollars of Longarm's money before disappearing with a chorus of wild, triumphant howls.

"I made them leave you the two best outlaws' horses," Longarm said to the couple. "And Holly, I'm glad we were able to return your stolen eight hundred dollars."

"Guess they never had a place to spend it out here," Holly said. "But what about you?"

"I may have to wire Billy for additional travel funds," Longarm replied. "But I've still got the buckskins that I can redeem for cash back in Laramie. They should bring enough for train fare to Denver."

Frenchy stuck out his hand. "I doubt we'll ever ride the trail together again, my good friend."

Longarm was hoping this was true. "Just change your name and be loving and loyal to Holly."

"And we'll name our first son after you," she added with a shy smile. "You'll get an anonymous announcement of the event."

"I'd like that." Longarm planted his foot in his stirrup and swung onto his horse. He studiously dallied the lead rope of his second buckskin around his saddlehorn before looking down at the radiant couple. He couldn't hide the fact that he was jealous as hell of Frenchy.

"Who said that there is any justice in life that a man like you should win a prize like that?" he asked with a half smile as he reined away before they started lovey-dovin' again.

Watch for

LONGARM AND THE GOLDEN DEATH

178th in the bold LONGARM series
from Jove

Coming in October!

If you enjoyed this book, subscribe now and get...

TWO FREE

A $7.00 VALUE—